THE SILENT DRIVER

A NOVEL INSPIRED BY TRUE EVENTS

ORLANDUS SHORTER

The Silent Driver

A Novel Inspired By True Events

By Orlandus Shorter

Published by The Legacy Group

© 2026 Orlandus Shorter

First Edition -- January 2026

Printed in the United States of America

ISBN (Paperback): 978-1-970955-00-2

ISBN (eBook): 978-1-970955-02-6

ISBN (Hardback): 978-1-970955-01-9

Cover and Interior design by Orlandus Shorter

The Legacy Group Houston, Texas

To my LEGACY

Shantel, Shatara, Tatyana, Iman, Michael, and My Dreame —
*You mean more to me than these words can express. You're the reason I
do what I do. I am proud to share this moment with you. I loved you on
your first breath, and I'll love you on my last.*

*To my mother, **Helen F. Shorter** (RIP) — You are the light to my
darkest day. Thank you for loving me beyond measure and showing us
strength even on your weakest days. You are forever in my heart.*

*To my **Dad** — Thank you for being you. You showed me what hard
work looks like. Even when life happens, you continue to show up and
be diligent. Your resilience is unmatched. I love you, Doc.*

CONTENTS

INTRODUCTION

Read This Before You Ride

Listen. Before we get rolling, let me give you the lowdown on who you're riding with.

My name is on the cover, but in here I'm the Silent Driver. That's how I roll. I drive. I listen. I watch. And I keep my mouth shut, until now.

I've had CEOs slide into my backseat like kings. I've had rookies fresh off a contract, hands still shaking from their first million. I've had hardcore rappers who couldn't stop apologizing, and women who didn't feel like saying sorry to anybody. I've heard arguments that ended marriages and confessions that saved a few. I've seen tears hit leather and lies float like farts.

People talk in the car. They do more than talk, sometimes. Something about rolling down a highway with the city whispering around you makes folks feel safe. Makes them feel alive. They forget about me and the mirror. This makes me the ultimate fly on the wall.

These stories? Some happened exactly like I tell them with the names and places bent just enough to keep mother fuckers from suing me. Some are stitched together, a little bit of this ride, a little bit of that one. Because what matters is the truth inside the story.

And a few? Well... even I'm not sure if those were real, or if the road just made them up for me while I was headed home at two in the morning. You be the judge.

Here's all you really need to know: I don't talk while I'm driving, unless I'm being spoken to. But when the engine's off and it's just me and you? Just keep our secrets just that, between me and you.

Buckle up.

– The Silent Driver, Houston, Texas

ONE
THE FIRST FARE

You ever step into a new life, and it still smells like the dealership? That was me, that night at Bush Intercontinental, sitting behind the wheel of a black Escalade so fresh the plastic was still tucked in the side pockets. Houston heat doing pushups on the windshield. Planes floating in and out like slow-moving stars. I was early on purpose, nerves dressed up, hiding the nervousness.

But let me back up a second, because the ride didn't start at the terminal.

It started six months earlier, in a conference room at a major airline, HR Department, where I sat across from my manager holding a piece of paper that looked like a joke.

"2.8%," I said, staring at the number.

She smiled like she was doing me a favor. "I can't give you more," she said. "You already make more than everyone on the floor. Hell, you almost make more than me."

I'm thinking, hell, I should be making more than you, but I opted to smile and just say thank you. I did the math in my head. Came out to about seventy dollars more per paycheck. Before taxes.

I'd spent the last year working in HR for this company. I was over the background checks for the flight attendants joining the company. I personally handled over 6,000 background checks that year. I showed up early, stayed late, answered emails at midnight because someone gave me a fishing license, faking as if it was a driver's license. I was shooting for the holy grail: Exceeds Expectations.

And this was what exceeding expectations got me.

Seventy dollars.

I walked out of that meeting knowing two things. One, they liked me. Two, they were never gonna pay me what I was worth.

Cool. I don't need a war. I need a plan.

So, at night I started driving Uber. Not just for the money, though it helped, but to learn Houston. This city doesn't give you a neat little grid like Chicago. It sprawls like it's running from itself. Beltway, 610, Westpark, 59 that still wants to be 69. Houston will test your memory and your brakes.

I learned by getting lost, then pretending I meant it. I learned by watching where the money slept. I learned the difference between a Montrose coffee run and a River Oaks "don't ask questions." I learned which neighborhoods tipped and which ones acted like you should be grateful they got in your car at all.

But more than that, I learned how to read people better. How to tell when someone wanted to talk and when they needed silence. How to spot trouble before it climbed in. How to make a stranger feel safe enough to tell you things they wouldn't tell their own family.

I was good at it. Better than I expected to be.

And that's when I realized: I didn't need the airline. I needed my own business.

Now, my father's been in the limo game for years. Owns his own service. You're probably wondering why I didn't just start working under his banner. That's a whole different story for a different day, and we'll get there. But I knew I needed my own ride. My own name. My own reputation. I'm leaving my "good ole' fancy HR job," and not to work for someone else.

Still, he's my father. When I told him I was leaving the airline to go full-time, he didn't lecture me. Didn't tell me I was making a mistake. He just said, "You ready?"

"I'm ready."

He nodded. "Then let's see if you can handle the real ones."

A week later, he called me.

"Pickup at Bush," he said, like he was handing me the keys to my own ride. "Husband and wife. International flight. Piney Point. Don't be late. Don't be green."

"I stay clean, I'm never green," I told him.

He laughed like he knew better. "We'll see."

So now picture me that night: parked in the limo lot at Bush Intercontinental, engine purring low, AC fighting the humidity like it had a personal grudge. I wiped a smudge off the chrome that only I could see. Checked my phone for the flight info.

The Pinkermans. London Heathrow to Houston. Terminal E. Landed.

I took a sip of water. Checked my tie in the mirror. Straightened my collar. This wasn't just a ride. This was my audition. My reputation was on the line, and if I messed this up, I wouldn't just lose a client. I'd lose respect.

I grabbed my phone and created a sign through an app: PINKERMAN in clean block letters. Stepped out into the thick Houston night and headed inside.

Arrivals at Bush after midnight is its own kind of theater. Soldiers coming home to families who'd been counting days. Grandmas clapping for nobody in particular. Business travelers dragging roller bags like they were hauling their own exhaustion.

Drivers stood shoulder to shoulder with signs in their hands, a lineup of names that meant nothing to anyone except the person looking for them, or the people passing by thinking somehow you are security.

I found my spot, held up my sign, and waited.

That's when I saw her.

Shorter than I expected. Athletic build, like she lived in a gym or used to. Pale skin with beads of sweat already forming on her forehead even though the terminal AC was working overtime. She wore a crisp white blouse, dark fitted skirt, heels that clicked on the tile with authority. Her perfume hit me before she did, clean and sharp, not sweet or floral. Something that smelled like it was expensive.

No husband in sight. Just her.

She looked at me as if she recognized her name.

"Mrs. Pinkerman?" I said, holding the sign steady.

She blinked at me, then at the sign, then back at me like she had to calibrate her eyes.

"Yes," she said. Her voice was clipped. British accent but softened by years somewhere else. "My husband is detained. Customs. He told me not to wait."

"Of course," I said. "Let's get you home."

She handed me her carry-on, not heavy, but expensive heavy. The kind of leather that announces itself without saying a word. I took it, nodded toward the exit, and led the way.

Outside, the Houston night hit us both in the face. Heat doesn't ease up for anyone, not even at midnight.

I opened the rear passenger door. She slid into the back seat, leaned her head against the headrest, and let out a long breath like she'd been holding it since London.

I closed her in, walked around, loaded her bag in the back, and climbed into the driver's seat. The Escalade became its own little country. Cool air. Soft leather. The hum of the engine like a lullaby.

"Temperature okay?" I asked, catching her eyes in the rearview.

"Perfect."

"There's water in the console if you need it."

"Thank you."

She reached into the rear center console, pulled out a cold bottle, twisted the cap, and took a long drink. I didn't stare. Just adjusted the mirror, checked my route, and pulled out of the lot.

Five minutes passed with nothing but that water bottle taking small hits and her breathing settling down. I kept it smooth. No hard brakes. No excessive speeding. I remembered something my father used to tell me when I was learning: put an empty can on the dashboard. If you can drive without it flying off, at any speed, you know you're rolling smooth. He was right. You don't play around with the wheel and somebody else's life. Mess around and you'll wake up dead, and shit, I had things to do tomorrow.

We merged onto the freeway. The city slid by in bright little pieces. A billboard with some lawyer calling himself The Hammer. A gas station where somebody was about to make a life-changing decision. A strip center with a club that had probably saved more marriages than therapy. I know my town.

Mrs. Pinkerman didn't say a word. Just sat back there, drinking her water, staring out the window like she was trying to remember what country she was in.

Ten minutes passed. Then fifteen.

The silence wasn't uncomfortable. It was the good kind. The kind that says I trust you enough not to fill the air with bullshit.

I kept my eyes on the road. Hands at ten and two. Lane changes smooth as butter.

Then I noticed something shift.

When she shifted in the seat, a couple of buttons on her blouse popped open, revealing what my uncle would've called a pair of full-grown dogs tucked under her chin. Like she could just stand there, lay her plate on those bad boys, and eat her dinner. High. Proud. Sitting like they'd never met gravity. I kept my hands at ten and two and my eyes mostly forward, the road stretching out clean under Memorial, but her nipples at nine and three. A lot of women would kill for that kind of posture. She didn't show them off; they just showed up.

Her breathing changed. Not panicked. Not distressed. Just... different. Focused.

I took another glance in the mirror, quick, professional, and saw her adjust herself in the seat.

I kept my eyes forward.

I thought to myself, mind your business, drive the car, and get her home. She's just unwinding. Nothing to see here. I laughed to myself.

But then I heard it. A gentle vibration like a soft hum. A soft exhale. A pause. Another shift in the leather.

I didn't look. Didn't need to. My mind was racing because I'm like, What the fuck? But not in a freaked-out way. I was a little turned on. Hell, who am I kidding; this lady had breasts the size of two firm cantaloupes and she's masturbating behind me. I was losing my mind. Trying to stay focused, wondering if she's going to ask me to pull over or come in after I get to her house. Oh, this lady is married, I can't do that, as though I was invited into the session. It's amazing how many different directions your mind can go when you are experiencing something out of the norm. When someone forgets the mirror or maybe simply doesn't care.

I'm also impressed at the level of control she has and how quiet her moans were. Amazing.

Memorial Drive stretched out clean and empty. The next exit was still a couple miles out. The music played low, something instrumental I kept in rotation for nights like this. Some dude named The Sutradhar. Weird name, nice grooves.

Out of nowhere, I hit a pothole, and Mrs. Pinkerman lost it. She screamed and howled like a wolf at the moon with extreme delight. Her body shook uncontrollably and watching her try to hold on to the arm bar above her head was a sight to see. I gripped the wheel tighter, eyes locked forward, praying to God we didn't hit another one. Because if we did, I might crash this SUV my damn self.

I can't believe this is happening. I think I just pinched my own nipple. But I kept my face neutral. Kept my hands steady. Kept driving like nothing had happened. Because in a way, nothing had.

She pulled her scarf out of her purse once she gathered herself, wiping her face first, then the rest. Then my seat, well, she just smeared shit around on my seat because that little scarf was not going to pick up anything, and from the sound of things, there was a lot.

I did say this was my FIRST ride as my own business, didn't I?

The gate to her estate came up on the left. I slowed, turned in, and followed the long driveway that probably had its own ZIP code. Big house. Lights off except for the porch. Quiet. Expensive quiet.

I pulled up to the front door, put the car in park, and stepped out.

She was already adjusting her purse, checking her phone, putting her professional face back on. I opened her door, stepped back, and gave her space.

"Let me grab your bag," I said.

"Thank you," she said softly. Her voice was lighter now. Calmer.

I pulled her luggage from the back and set it down by the front door. She walked up beside me, pulled out a slim wallet, and peeled off three hundred-dollar bills like it was loose change.

She pressed them into my hand. Her fingers were warm.

"For you," she said. "And for the quiet."

I looked her in the eye. Steady. Professional.

"Yes ma'am," I said. "Always."

She gave me the smallest smile, then disappeared behind her door.

I walked back to the Escalade, climbed in, and just sat there for a minute under the cabin light.

Three hundred dollars cash in my hand. A cleaning fee that would hit my account tomorrow, yes, she's definitely getting charged a cleaning fee. And a brand-new leather seat that would never be quite the same.

I started the engine, pulled out of that long driveway, and headed back toward the city.

People do all kinds of things in the backseat. They cry. They argue. They make confessions. They kiss. They grieve. They celebrate. And sometimes, they just... handle their business.

My job is to get them where they're going. Not to remember. Not to judge. Not to tell.

That's what the Silent Driver means.

That night taught me everything I needed to know about this business.

People don't hire you just to drive them. They hire you to hold space. To not flinch. To not judge. To let them be whoever they need to be for thirty minutes, and then to forget you ever saw it.

Some drivers can't do that. They talk too much. They pry. They make it weird. They turn a private moment into a story they tell at barbecues.

Not me.

I'm the Silent Driver.

I see everything. I say nothing. And I get paid for both.

That first fare? It set the tone for every ride that came after.

Some passengers need a therapist. Some need a witness. Some just need to get from point A to point B without anyone asking questions.

And me? I'm there for all of it.

Because silence isn't just about keeping secrets.

It's about respect.

It's about trust.

And sometimes, it's about knowing that the best thing you can do for someone is let them ride in peace.

TWO
BABY GOT BACK

My phone lit up with a booking I almost didn't take. Pickup in River Oaks. Drop-off at a hospice on the south side. Middle of the afternoon on a Tuesday. The kind of ride that didn't sit right on the inside before you even turn the key.

I pulled up to a house that looked like old, not as in ran over but vintage. Big, but not flashy. Brick. Neat lawn. Three cars in the driveway, a Lexus, a BMW, and a Tesla. All new. All expensive. None of them moving.

The front door opened and a woman in her fifties stepped out. Blonde hair pulled back tight. Yoga pants and a fleece jacket. She looked tired in that specific way people look when they've been tired for years.

Behind her came a man about the same age. Polo shirt. Khakis. The kind of guy who plays golf on Saturdays and complains about his taxes. He had his phone out, already halfway into another conversation before he'd finished this one.

And between them, moving slower than the hour hand on a clock, was Mr. Kraken.

Ninety if he was a day. Maybe older. Hard to tell with some folks; life wears them down so much they stop counting. He was thin, the kind of thin that makes you think of hospital gowns and meal trays left untouched. Wrinkled suit that had probably fit him twenty pounds ago. Tie twisted like someone else had tied it and he'd been too tired to fix it. His glasses fogged up the second he stepped into the Houston heat.

"Dad, you sure about this?" the woman said, not looking at him.

"I'm sure," he said. Voice like dry paper.

"We could take you," the man said, but his thumb was already scrolling. "I just have a meeting at three."

"It's fine," Mr. Kraken said. "I called a car."

The woman glanced at me, then back at her father. "You have your phone?"

"I have my phone."

"Call if you need anything."

"I will."

But we all knew he wouldn't.

I stepped forward. "Mr. Kraken?"

He looked at me and nodded, grateful that someone had said his name like it still meant something.

I opened the back door. The woman handed me a small suitcase, old leather, corners rubbed raw like it had been around the world twice. It looked older than me and should have retired years ago.

"He wants this in the back seat with him," she said. "Not the trunk."

"No problem."

Mr. Kraken slid into the seat with the careful movements of a man who'd learned not to trust his own body. I positioned the suitcase behind my seat where he could see it. The woman leaned in, kissed him on the forehead, quick, obligatory, and stepped back.

"Love you, Dad," she said.

"Love you too, sweetheart."

The man gave a wave without looking up from his phone.

I closed the door.

As I walked around to the driver's side, I caught the woman and the man already heading back inside. No standing on the porch. No watching him leave. Just gone. Like he was already a memory they were trying not to think about.

I climbed in, adjusted the mirror, and glanced back.

"Where to, sir?"

He gave me the address. A hospice off MLK. I knew it. Unfortunately, this happens more than you would believe.

"Can you take the long way?" he asked, voice quiet but firm. "Through Fifth Ward. Lyons Avenue. Quitman. Slow, if you don't mind."

I nodded. "No problem, sir."

That's one thing about driving, you learn real quick that time belongs to whoever's spending their money. And the way he said it, slow wasn't about traffic. It was something totally different.

He leaned back, folded his hands on that small suitcase, and stared out the window.

I pulled away from the house. In the rearview, I saw the driveway empty. Three cars sitting there like monuments to people too busy to say goodbye.

We drove in silence for the first ten minutes. Mr. Kraken didn't look at me, didn't ask questions, didn't make small talk. He just watched Houston roll by like he was reading a book he'd memorized but wanted to see one more time.

He looked like he had to be every bit of ninety years old, but he was an old white dude so he was probably sixty. Aw hush, you were thinking it. I'm just telling it like it is. Let me finish my story. I'm The Silent Driver, you be The Silent Reader and relax.

Where was I? Yeah, frail man like I said before. But his eyes, his eyes were alive. Bright. Scanning like he was reading the city out loud to himself. He smelled like medicine, old books, and mothballs, the kind of scent that tells you he'd been through more hospitals than vacations.

I took the long route through Midtown, then cut east toward Fifth Ward. The buildings started to change. Glass towers gave way to old shotgun houses. Coffee shops turned into corner stores with bars on the windows. The Houston he was looking for was still here, but it was buried under new paint and FOR SALE signs.

We rolled down Lyons Avenue, and that's when he started pointing.

Not at me. At the air. At the past. At His-story.

"That's where we met," he said when we passed a boarded-up diner.

I slowed down. The building was gutted. Windows broken. Faded sign hanging crooked: Dot's Kitchen. Someone had spray-painted over it, but you could still see the letters underneath.

"You spilled coffee on my shoes," he said, voice soft, like he was talking to her and not me. "I didn't even care."

He chuckled, a sound that came from somewhere deep and forgotten.

"She had on a yellow dress. Looked like sunshine walked into that place. I bought her breakfast to apologize. Eggs, bacon, toast. She ate every bite and told me I owed her another meal to make it even." He paused. "We got married six months later."

I glanced at him in the mirror. His hand was pressed flat against the window, fingers spread like he was trying to reach through the glass and touch the memory.

A mile later, we passed a cell phone store. Bright LED sign. Posters in the window advertising prepaid plans. But underneath the cheap paint job, you could still see the bones of what it used to be, the classic red-and-white barber pole embedded in the brick, the old-fashioned door frame, the tile floor visible through the glass.

"That used to be my shop," Mr. Kraken whispered.

I stopped the car. Put it in park. Let him look.

"Kraken's Barbershop," he said. "Had it for thirty years. Taught my boys how to cut hair in there. Thought if I taught them to work with their hands, it would keep them honest."

He went quiet.

"Didn't work out that way."

I didn't ask what he meant. Didn't need to. The bitterness in his voice said enough.

"They don't talk to you much, do they?" I said, careful.

He shook his head. "Not much. Not anymore."

"I'm sorry, sir."

He waved a hand, dismissive. "It's alright. People grow apart. Life gets busy. I get it."

But I could tell he didn't get it. And it still hurt.

I put the car back in drive and rolled forward.

We turned onto Quitman, and he tapped the glass.

"Stop here."

I pulled over in front of a massive oak tree. It sat in the middle of a vacant lot, gnarled and ancient, branches stretching out like it was holding up the sky. The trunk was so wide three people couldn't wrap their arms around it. It had survived hurricanes. Harvey, Ike, Rita. Outlived the neighborhood around it.

"Kids played tag right under that tree," Mr. Kraken said, staring. "Lord, the noise they made. Thought it would never end."

He smiled, but it didn't reach his eyes.

"This was back when people knew their neighbors. Back when you could leave your door unlocked. Back when this place was..." He trailed off. "Different."

I thought about what he wasn't saying. About how Fifth Ward used to be his, back when it was white, back before the city shifted and changed and he moved out to River Oaks with his family and his money. About how he was mourning a version of Houston that didn't mourn him back.

But I didn't say that. Some thoughts you keep to yourself.

"Do you remember?" he whispered, still staring at the tree.

I didn't answer. The question wasn't for me.

We kept driving. He pointed out more stops, and I took them all.

A church. Boarded up now, windows covered with plywood, front steps cracked and weeds growing through the concrete.

"Got married there," he said. "Buried my parents there. My brother. Thought I'd be buried there too."

A liquor store that he said used to be a hardware store. His hardware store.

"Sold it in '89," he said. "Thought I was getting a good deal. Guy who bought it flipped it six months later for twice what he paid me."

He laughed, but it was hollow.

"Guess I wasn't as smart as I thought."

A street corner. Nothing special. Just a regular intersection with a stop sign and a bus shelter.

He went quiet when we got there. Didn't point. Didn't explain. Just stared for a full minute.

Finally, he spoke.

"Lost a friend here. Long time ago. Shouldn't have been out that night."

That's all he said.

I let the silence sit. Let him have his moment. Then I eased through the intersection and kept driving.

About twenty minutes into the ride, he sat up straighter. His eyes cleared. A smile broke through the fog of memory and medicine.

"Baby Got Back!" he said, loud and sudden.

I blinked. "Sir?"

He laughed, really laughed, for the first time all ride. The sound filled the car like light breaking through clouds.

"That's what I used to say to my wife. Beth Ann Kraken. BAK. Baby Got Back."

I couldn't help it. I joined in the laugh.

"She hated that joke," he said, still laughing. "Threatened to divorce me every time I said it. But I'd catch her smiling when she thought I wasn't looking. She'd shake her head and call me ridiculous, but she never stopped me."

His voice softened.

"Been gone eight years now. Feels like yesterday. Feels like forever."

I watched him in the mirror. The smile faded. The light went out of his eyes. He deflated back into the seat, the memory slipping away like water through his fingers.

"She was the best thing that ever happened to me," he said quietly. "And I didn't realize it until she was gone."

I nodded. "Yes, sir."

We drove the rest of the way in silence.

The hospice sat at the end of a quiet street, tucked behind a row of trees like it was trying to hide. It was clean. Modern. The kind of place that tried too hard to look welcoming, soft lighting, fake plants in the windows, a wooden sign out front with cheerful letters that said New Horizons Care Center.

But it didn't matter how nice they made it look. It was still a place people went to die.

I pulled up to the front entrance and put the car in park. Turned off the engine. The sudden quiet felt weighted.

Mr. Kraken didn't move right away. He just sat there, staring at the building like it might disappear if he waited long enough.

"We're here, sir," I said gently.

"I know."

I got out, walked around, and opened his door. He swung his legs out slow, gripping the frame for balance. I offered my hand. He took it, and I felt how cold his fingers were, how weak his grip.

He stood, wobbling for a second, then steadied himself.

I reached in for the suitcase. He stopped me.

"I got it," he said.

"You sure?"

"I'm sure."

He picked it up with both hands, holding it against his chest like it was the only thing keeping him upright.

The front door opened, and a nurse stepped out. Middle-aged, kind eyes, scrubs with little flowers on them. She smiled like she'd done this a thousand times.

"Mr. Kraken," she said warmly. "We've been expecting you."

He nodded.

She reached for the suitcase. "Let me take that for you."

He hesitated, then let her. Watched it go like he was watching his whole life disappear through that door.

Before he followed her inside, he turned back to me. Looked me in the eye.

"You didn't ask questions," he said. "I appreciate that."

"No sir."

He nodded slowly. "Most people need to fill the silence. You let me have mine."

"Yes, sir."

He extended his hand. I shook it. His grip was firmer this time.

"Thank you for the tour," he said, voice cracking. "It meant more than you know."

"Anytime, sir."

The nurse waited at the door. Mr. Kraken took a breath, straightened his twisted tie one last time, and walked inside.

Slow. Shuffling. But with his head up.

The door closed behind him, and it felt final.

I stood there for a minute. Didn't get back in the car right away. Just stood there, staring at the building, hands in my pockets.

I thought about his family. The three cars in the driveway. The daughter who kissed him out of obligation. The son who couldn't look up from his phone. The house they'd go back to tonight, and the empty chair at the table they wouldn't talk about.

I thought about Mr. Kraken's baby with back, Beth Ann. About how love outlives everything, even the person you loved. About how Mr. Kraken had spent the last hour of his freedom driving through a city that didn't remember him, saying goodbye to a life that was already over except for the paperwork.

I thought about the suitcase. What was in it? Photos? Letters? A yellow dress? Nothing at all?

I'd never know. And that was okay. Some stories aren't yours to finish.

I walked back to the car. Sat in the driver's seat. Didn't start the engine. Just sat.

The hospice door stayed closed. No movement. No sound.

I wondered if his family would visit. Wondered if they'd feel guilty when he was gone, or relieved. Wondered if he cared anymore, or if that ride through Fifth Ward was his way of letting go, not of life, but of the people who'd already let go of him.

After a while, I started the engine and pulled away.

I drove back through Fifth Ward. The streets looked different now. Emptier. Like the ghosts had gone with him.

Dot's Kitchen still boarded up.

The barbershop still a cell phone store.

The oak tree still standing, holding up the sky.

I thought about Mr. Kraken sitting in that hospice room right now, staring at a wall, holding that old suitcase in his lap. I thought about him whispering Baby Got Back to a woman who'd been gone eight years. I thought about how some people spend their whole lives trying to get back to a moment they can't name, and how the closest they ever get is a slow drive through a neighborhood that doesn't know their name anymore.

Some people hire you to drive them somewhere.

Some people hire you to let them say goodbye.

That day, I was both.

I never saw Mr. Kraken again. Never got a call from his family. Never saw his name in an obituary, though I looked.

But every now and then when I drive through Fifth Ward now, I think about him. About Beth Ann in her yellow dress. About the oak tree and the barbershop and the corner where he lost a friend.

About how we all carry suitcases full of things we can't let go of, even when our hands are too weak to hold them anymore.

And I think about silence. About how sometimes the kindest thing you can do for someone is let them live in their own world for a little while longer.

Some rides change your night.

Some change your week.

That one? That one stays with me.

THREE

THE PROXY

It was close to 11 p.m. when I should have shut the app off and gone home. I had already done three airport runs and a corporate dinner pickup.

Good night. Clean money.

The kind of Friday that reminds you why you started this business.

My back was tired, my eyes were heavy, and I had a DVR full of shows I had been meaning to watch for two months.

But I kept the app on.

Not because I needed another fare. I didn't.

But because sometimes the best clients come from accidents.

A stranger who needs discretion.

A regular in the making.

Someone who appreciates a driver who knows when to talk and when to disappear.

That is how I tell myself it is not about the money.

It is about control. About being the one who decides when the night ends.

Then the ping came in.

Friday night in Houston has a different feel.

Heat holds on to the pavement long after the sun clocks out.

Neon leaks from bar signs and paints the sidewalks in colors that do not exist in daylight.

Sirens talk to each other from different parts of the city like cousins shooting the shit on the phone.

I should have been off the clock.

I own a limo company.

I have regulars who book in advance, who just want to ride, in and out, airport runs, corporate events, or nights on the town.

Some nights I still flip that Uber Black app on.

Not because I need it.

Because every once in a while, a stranger sits down and turns into a client who respects quiet and pays on time.

If the ride makes sense, I hand a card and tomorrow they call me direct.

The ping came in on McKinney.

The towers along that run catch whatever light is left and spit it back at the street.

Glass for days.

I eased the Escalade up to the curb.

Paint looked wet under the lamps.

Leather still held the last detailers clean.

The cabin smelled like cedar and citrus.

You could feel the air sit right.

He came out of the building with his head down, moving like a man who is used to doors opening before he touches them.

Patagonia vest. White shirt that had never seen sweat.

Jeans with a careful fade. Sneakers too clean for any Houston sidewalk that had ever known rain.

He did not look at me.

Just slipped in behind the passenger seat and placed his phone on the leather, face up, like it was part of his outfit.

"River Oaks," he said.

Then he leaned in a little.

"Actually, let us just drive for a bit. I need to think. I will pay for the time."

People say that when they want to be alone without being alone.

Most of them are drunk or heartbroken.

He was neither.

His voice had no shake in it.

His eyes did not flinch.

He gave it like a man booking a conference room.

I nodded and pulled out.

Downtown fell into the mirrors in pieces of gold and blue.

We slid across the 45 and took Memorial.

Buffalo Bayou was a dark ribbon on my left.

Runners still moved under the lights along the path, their steps soft from up here.

The night had that heavy air that sticks to your skin.

In the cabin, the air stayed cool and dry.

A small mercy I can control.

He did not look out the window.

He sat back with his knees slightly apart and his hands lightly touching.

Every two or three minutes he checked his watch.

Not like a man who is late. Like a man syncing himself to a plan.

His left hand kept rubbing the inside of his right wrist where a band or a ring might have rested once.

No ring now.

No mark on the knuckles.

Nails clean.

Skin pale under the watch.

That told me he had not seen sunlight in a while.

I have learned to read temperature.

Fear runs hot, sweaty palms, shallow breathing, eyes that will not settle.

Grief runs cold, heavy shoulders, hands that do not know where to go.

But this was different.

This was practiced calm, the kind you work on in the mirror until your face believes the lie your mouth is telling.

I did not like it.

But I also did not have a reason not to like it.

He was not rude. Not drunk. Not doing anything wrong.

Just sitting there, watching his phone like he was waiting for a specific moment.

That is what bothered me most. Something just didn't feel right with this joker.

He was not anxious. He was ready.

I have driven cheaters who tried on honesty like a coat they could not afford.

Dealers who smelled like courage until the blue lights show up and they turn to chumps.

Pastors who practiced tough conversations in a whisper before a funeral.

You sit in this seat long enough and intention starts to have a temperature.

His felt cold and steady.

"Quiet enough to think?" I asked, just to hear how he handled small talk.

"Perfect," he said.

He smiled at the back of my head like we had already agreed on something.

The phone lit once.

He did not move.

It lit again.

He looked down at it, then away, like a street performer he did not want to encourage.

We floated past the Wortham, its curved roof sitting like a dark shell.

Downtown softened behind us.

Allen Parkway opened wide.

Couples crossed at long lights, laughing like they were the only ones in love in Houston.

He had the look of a man who has never been followed around a store in his life.

That clean-cut kind of confidence that gets called leadership in boardrooms and charm at country clubs.

Me, I am a six-foot-two Black man in a black truck.

We already looked like a headline waiting for a photograph.

He was staring at his phone now, not the screen but his reflection.

Checking his face.

Making sure the mask fit right.

That is when I knew for sure.

Something was wrong.

Not danger, performance.

Like I was watching a rehearsal for a scene I had not been cast in yet.

My stomach tightened.

Hands gripped the wheel.

I thought about ending the ride, but what would I say?

You are too calm, sir. Too composed. I do not like the vibe.

That is not a reason.

That is paranoia.

So, I kept driving.

The phone lit a third time, and he let it ring.

The fourth time, he answered.

Tapped speaker.

Set it in his lap.

Screen glow hitting his face.

"Hello," he said.

The voice that came through was tight and climbing.

"Mr. Evans, this is security at Montrose Tower. There has been an incident. It is your wife. I am so sorry. You need to get here now."

My hands tightened.

He did not choke. Did not shout.

He gave me a pause that lasted just long enough to sound believable.

Not long enough to sound fake.

"What are you talking about," he said, slow, like stepping into cold water.

"Is she okay?"

I have heard panic before.

Real panic does not have rhythm.

This did.

This was performance.

And I was his audience.

Or worse, his prop. I couldn't tell at this point.

"Please come now," the voice said. "Police are on the way."

He hung up and looked at me through the mirror.

The look said we understand each other.

His face knew where to put the sadness.

"Oh my God," he said. "My wife. Please. Montrose Tower. Go now."

I went.

The pedal dropped and the truck moved smooth.

I hit the lines no one else saw.

Lights turned green like they had rehearsed it.

But my mind was racing faster than the wheels.

A Black driver.

A white man in a panic.

A black truck.

A crime scene waiting.

We were a rolling stereotype with a GPS.

And the worst part, I could not do anything about it.

Could not pull over. Could not refuse.

What if I was wrong?

What if she really was hurt?

Then I am the driver who let a man's wife die because I did not feel right.

But if I was right, then I was delivering a murderer to his story.

Either way, I lose.

He did not call anyone back.

Did not text.

Did not even breathe heavy.

I looked down.

The Uber app still ticking.

Timestamps do not lie.

Thirty minutes in.

He had been with me the whole time.

He was not going to Montrose Tower.

He was building an alibi with a motherfucker that mute.

Montrose Tower came into view, red and blue reflections crawling up the glass.

Police tape fluttering.

Crowds forming.

Hotel glow making the grief look colder.

"Right to the entrance," he said, touching my shoulder.

"Where the cameras can see."

My own thought was louder.

Where the cops can see me.

Hands at ten and two.

Face neutral.

Body still.

A Black man at a white woman's tragedy is either a witness or a suspect.

And that line is drawn by someone else.

He stepped out, calm.

Not too fast.

Not too slow.

Perfect tragedy pacing. This bastard need a daytime Emmy win for best performance.

Someone called his name.

He walked toward them like the camera was already rolling.

Nobody looked at the driver.

Cops shifted cars.

Firemen talked low.

A woman cried into her hands.

The grief was real.

So was my fear.

I parked, shut off the engine, and checked my ride log.

Time in. Time out. Route saved.

If it ever came down to it, I had proof.

The app knows.

The car knows.

And so do I.

A text came through.

Nearby incident. Expect delays.

I laughed once, sharp and dry.

Yeah, no fucking kidding.

You can tell the truth and still ruin your life.

You can stay silent and let someone else's lie live on.

That is the math drivers like me do after midnight.

He came back thirty minutes later.

No tears.

Face set.

Knocked on the window.

"Thank you for getting me here," he said.

"Add another hour to the fare. For the trouble."

"No trouble," I said.

"You were with me the whole time. Right?"

"I was driving you," I said. "The whole time."

He nodded. "Right."

Left a thick envelope on the door.

Walked away.

I did not touch it.

Not then.

Just added it later to the glove box, where the lost things go.

Earrings. Cufflinks. A rosary.

Things passengers leave behind when truth gets too heavy.

On the drive out, the radio switched to news.

A woman had fallen from a high balcony.

No names released.

Police investigating.

I turned the volume down and stared at the road.

I thought about calling it in.

About walking into a station.

About how that would look, me explaining this story to a detective who already has a headline written.

Sir, are you sure what you heard was staged?

Sir, you know your dashcam does not record audio, right?

Sir, where were you when you pulled over near the park?

Every question ending in me.

So I did not call.

Because I knew this world is not built for proxies like me.

It is built for motherfuckers like him.

I drove until sunrise.

The sky went from purple to gray.

The air cooled.

At a red light, I opened my notes and typed:

Montrose Tower. 8:41 to 9:12. Four calls. On the fourth he answered on speaker. He asked for the cameras.

Then I stopped typing.

Because memory lies.

It edits itself to keep you sane.

I saved it anyway.

Locked the phone.

Drove on.

When I passed Montrose Tower again, the tape was gone.

Just glass, guards, and silence.

A building that had swallowed a story whole.

I spoke out loud to no one.

He did not need a driver.

He needed a proxy.

The words sat in the cabin like another passenger.

Then they settled into the dark.

I drove home as the sun came up.

Windows down.

Air cool on my face.

The note stayed in my phone.

The money stayed in the glove box.

And the question stayed in my mind.

What do you do when telling the truth might destroy you, and staying silent might destroy someone else?

I did not have an answer.

All I knew was that every time I pick up a fare, I am not just driving them somewhere.

I am holding their secrets, their lies, their truths.

And sometimes, I am holding the weight of what I cannot prove and cannot forget.

That is the job.

That is the cost.

And that is why, six months later, when I saw his face on the news, cleared of all charges and moving to a new city with his late wife's insurance payout, I did not feel vindicated.

I just felt tired.

Because I was right.

And it did not matter.

.

FOUR
LANG JANG

Okay. So. You three chapters in now, and I been tryin' to hold it together. Keep it clean. Keep it professional. Write this thing like I'm applyin' for a damn job or somethin'.

But hell... I'm not at the airline sittin' in some cubicle. And we family now, right?

I don't have time to be fake with you. My code-switchin' days are over. And if I gotta be all stiff and proper with you, I'd rather keep my stories to myself.

At fifty, somethin' changed. My level of I-Don't-Give-a-Fuck hit an all-time high.

So with that bein' said, I'ma tell it the way I saw it.

Well, heard it.

Hell, experienced it.

You ready for this?

Hold on. Let me pour a drink.

You want one?

Aight then.

So I'm sittin' in my office, you know, the dining room table, lookin' at the schedule for tomorrow, seein' who's who.

Everything look regular until I see a name pop up. Lang Jang.

I had to blink twice. I thought the system glitched.

Sounded like somebody made that up just to test me.

Pickup: Bush Airport.

Drop-off: Post Oak.

2PM. Easy enough.

But when I tell you it's the middle of the day and the devil is waving at me on my windshield.

Houston in August, where the air feel like it's mad at you.

Plane lands, I'm outside waitin' in that heavy damn heat

Doors slide open, and here come this man. Bright jacket. Sunglasses. Walk like he got a drumline followin' him.

He waves before he even spots me.

"Lang Jang in the building!"

I pop the trunk, grab his carry-on. Little roller bag trailin' behind him like it's a French Poodle. I can already tell this is gonna be one of those rides.

He climbs in the back, phone to his ear.

"Yeah, yeah, Lang Jang just landed. Lang Jang gotta keep his head straight. Lang Jang been workin' too hard. Lang Jang hungry than a motherfucker Lang Jang need rest, yeah he do."

I glance up in the mirror. Yup. He serious.

Whole ride, dude talking with himself in the third person like he got a studio audience back there.

He'd ask himself a question, then answer it.

Laugh, then congratulate himself.

At one point he clapped.

Not for me. Not for anyone that I could see. This dude just clapped, like a real applause.

"That's good, Lang Jang, write that shit down!"

Now, I ain't gonna lie, the motherfucker was funny. Like, for real, for real.

I'm tryin' to keep a straight face 'cause clearly, he rehearsin', but then he hit this line about married folks arguin' in Target and I damn near lost it.

He catches me in the mirror.

"You laughin' at Lang Jang?"

I say, "No sir. Just clearin' my throat."

He nods, satisfied. "Good. You can laugh. Lang Jang don't do silence."

I'm thinkin', Dude, silence is literally my job.

And just as he continued his "phone conversation", his phone actually rings.

He looks down, blinks, then says, "Oh. Lang Jang signal musta dropped," and hangs up on nobody.

Now he riffin' about life, fame, airports that smell like wet fries, and the government hidin' extra Tuesdays from the calendar.

I'm sittin' there wonderin' if I should record him for Netflix or call somebody's hospital to pick him up.

We roll through downtown. He starts narrating every damn thing he see.

"Look at that mural, Lang Jang. That's culture right there. That's black excellence. Oh Black EXCELLENCE, I tell ya."

"That boy on that scooter don't love his life."

"Houston traffic, ha! that's the damn devil's marathon."

He keep goin'. And I'm not gonna lie, somewhere between I-10 and Westheimer, I start likin' the dude.

He ridiculous, but he harmless. And most times, harmless is a blessing.

We stop at a Whataburger drive-thru 'cause he "need fries to process existence."

He orders like he's on stage. "Lemme get a Number One for the Number One, no onions 'cause Lang Jang kiss with confidence!"

The girl on the intercom didn't know what the hell was going on. "what you say she kept asking."

He tips her forty dollars through the window, tells her, "Invest in yourself."

Then looks dead at me and says, "See, Big Dog, that's how you plant good karma."

I said, "That's how you get overdraft alerts."

He cracked up so hard he slapped the back seat.

I couldn't help but laugh too.

Now we back on the road, him munchin' fries, salt flyin' everywhere, talkin' about how fame's just high-definition loneliness.

He said it like it was a quote, so I looked at him through the mirror.

"You read that somewhere?"

He shook his head. "Nah. I lived that somewhere."

Silence filled the truck for the first time since the airport.

And it wasn't awkward, it was deep. Real deep.

That's when I realized maybe all that talkin' wasn't for show. Maybe that was survival.

Some people pray out loud. He just do it with punchlines.

We pull up to Post Oak, one of them spots that charge you for air.

He stops mid-sentence, leans up between the seats.

"Big Dog, you ever talk to yourself?"

I say, "Sometimes, yeah."

He nods slow. "Good. Means you trust the only person who really know what's goin' on."

Then he gets out, smooth as ever, tosses a crisp fifty in the front seat, and walks toward the lobby like he on a red carpet, hummin' that same rhythm he'd been talkin' in.

Left his bags, of course.

Tryin' to be cool, showin' out for whoever inside, struttin' around empty-handed like he shootin' a commercial.

I hop out, grab his luggage, jog up before valet snatches it.

He turns, grins like it was all part of the plan. "My man! Lang Jang appreciate you!"

I just shook my head. "You good, boss."

I get back in the truck. Door shuts. Silence.

Sitting there, AC hummin', wonderin' if I just witnessed a meltdown or a masterpiece.

Next afternoon I drop off a trip to the Post Oak and guess who flags me down outside the hotel like he been waiting on me the whole time.

Yup. Damn Lang Jang himself.

Bright yellow suit this time. No bag. Just vibes.

"Big Dog, I knew you would be back. You still drivin, Who else to pick up beside Lang Jang'?"

"I actually didn't have no more clients for the day and he wanted me for the rest of the day at $95 an hour, we can ride all day.

"Lang Jang been waiting on you" he says, climbin' in. "Lang Jang need a favor. Ain't about money, it's about destiny."

"Where we headin'?"

He points forward like he conducting a parade. "Let's ride till the truth show up."

Aight then. I put it in drive.

We start movin' down Post Oak, traffic thick as grits.

He's hummin' to himself again, this time quieter. Then he says, "You ever wonder what'd happen if you stopped pretendin' to be normal?"

I said, "Brother, I drive people for a livin'. Pretendin' to be normal is my job."

He laughed. "That's deep. Write that down. We both philosophers, just one of us got better shoes."

He had a point. His shoes looked like 2 months of my rent.

We cruised for a while, him talkin', me listenin'.

Turns out Lang Jang wasn't just talkin' to talk, he used to be a comedian. Opened for some names you'd recognize. Did shows out in L.A. till the world stopped clappin'. Then one night he bombed so bad he quit mid-set, walked off stage, bought a one-way to Houston, and never looked back.

"Stage broke me," he said. "But it also built me. You know what that mean?"

"Yeah," I said. "Means you still showin' up."

He smiled, quiet. "Exactly."

We made a few stops. Smoothie King, gas station, a pawn shop where he swore he left "a piece of his destiny" in 2019.

Everywhere we went, he talked to people like he already knew 'em.

Told the cashier she looked like "the sunshine after probation." Told a homeless vet his aura smelled like victory. Told me I drive like a jazz musician.

By the third stop I realized something, he wasn't crazy. He was awake.

Too awake.

Like most folks' brains got filters to protect 'em from too much reality. His didn't.

Everything hit him raw. That's why he talked so much. It was either that or explode.

Later that evening, we end up at Discovery Green. He gets out, takes his shoes off, walks straight across the grass, "Lang Jang be grounding" then he laughs.

Kids playin', lights comin' on, fountains dancin'.

He looks up at the sky and says, "Man, you ever notice how stars don't need promotion?"

I said, "What?"

"They just are, big dog. Just show up. Don't post. Don't brag. Don't schedule content. Just shine. And people look up 'cause they can't help it."

He looks over his shoulder at me. "You a star too, you just ain't forgivin' yourself enough to shine."

Where is he going with this I thought but let it go.

We sat there a while. He told me about his momma; how she worked nights cleanin' offices, leavin' him notes that said Keep laughin', boy. God listenin'.

He said every time he wanted to quit, he'd hear her voice say that again.

Then he pulled a crumpled notebook from his jacket pocket. Pages bent, ink smudged.

"This here's Lang Jang Volume Two," he said. "Volume One burned up in a Motel 6 fire. You believe in signs?"

"I believe in smoke detectors," I said.

He laughed so hard people turned around. Then he got quiet again.

"Life's funny," he said. "But only if you survive it long enough to laugh."

We sat there till the park lights flicked off. Then he said, "Alright, big dog, back to the Post Oak."

On the way, he dozed off mid-sentence, snorin' soft.

I looked at him and thought: this man can't even rest without performing. Even his dreams got an audience.

When we got back, he woke up just as we turned in.

"Good ride, big dog. You ever think about writin' a book?"

I said, "Funny you mention that."

He smiled. "When you do, make sure Lang Jang in Chapter Four. That number feels divine."

He got out, grabbed his bag this time, and turned back.

"You helped Lang Jang remember he still funny."

Then he walked inside, leavin' that notebook on the backseat.

I called out, "Hey, you forgot, " but the doors closed.

I picked up the notebook. On the front it said, "Laugh Before You Leave."

Inside, the first page read:

"Talking to yourself ain't crazy. It's self-maintenance."

I sat there, flippin' through them pages, half jokes, half prayers.

Lines about pain, purpose, old friends, lost shows. Stuff that felt too honest for a comedy set. Stuff that sounded like somebody tryin' to laugh their way outta drownin'.

One page just said: 'Mom, I'm still laughin'. Hope you still listenin'.

I thought about keepin' it. But I knew the book wasn't mine.

So next day, I drove back to Post Oak, asked concierge if a guest named Lang Jang checked out.

They said nobody by that name ever stayed there.

No address. The booking phone number disconnected, The guy is just... gone.

I sat in the truck a long time that afternoon.

Notebook on the seat.

City buzzin' around me.

And I realized maybe that's what he wanted, to leave it with somebody who'd listen.

So I keep that notebook in the glovebox now, next to the other things I don't know what to do with,

A wedding ring a bride forgot.

A lighter shaped like a cross.

A key that don't fit any lock I own.

All reminders of people who talk when they think no one's listenin'.

And truth be told? I been talkin' to myself lately too.

Just ain't brave enough to do it out loud.

FIVE
THE RECEPTIONIST

Now this one takes me back to the grind.

Back when I was out there practically beggin' folks to believe in my business before I really believed in it myself. When my shirts were pressed too hard, my voice was too high-pitched from the nerves, and my confidence was just somethin' I wore like a rented suit; looked good on the outside, but I knew it didn't fit right yet.

Those early days had a certain kind of hunger to 'em. The kind that don't come from ambition, it comes from fear. Fear of goin' back to broke. Fear of tellin' people you tried somethin' and it didn't work. Fear of hearin' your own voice say, "maybe you ain't built for this shit."

I was walkin' into offices with my little folder of rate sheets, dress shoes too new, suit too clean, heart beatin' too fast. If the lights were on, I was knockin'. Didn't matter what kind of business it was, dental, law, medical, tech, whatever. If they had people comin' and goin', I figured somebody needed a ride.

Sometimes I'd park outside a building, sit there five whole minutes, talkin' to myself before I went in. It allowed me to see how many Ubers or other limos were picking up or dropping off there on the regular. "Alright, be confident. Smile, don't grin. Don't talk too fast. Don't sound desperate. You got this shit," I'd say to myself; my own personal pep talk before the main event. Then I'd grab my folder, push through the doors, and pray they didn't see the nerves sittin' right behind my professionalism.

You learn a lot about people when you're sellin' yourself for a living. Most folks don't look up when you walk in. They hear your pitch but they don't listen. They look at your shoes before your eyes. You can tell how much power somebody thinks they got by how slow they flip your business card over. They try to gatekeep when they barely made it in their selves. I remember comin' home after a long day, droppin' my tie on the counter, thinkin' maybe I was crazy for tryin', but I wanted this to work, hell, it had to work. I put it all on the line. It's a lonely kind of grind, tryin' to convince the world you got somethin' worth payin' attention to when you're still tryna convince yourself.

One afternoon, I end up at this medical spot off Kirby. Fancy place. Quiet. Smelled like flowers and sanitizer but looked money. You could hear the air-conditioning before you saw the people. Marble floors that looked like they'd been polished by hand, magazines stacked just right, candles that probably cost more than my first week's profit.

I step in, straighten my tie, and see her behind the counter.

Now look, she ain't model-cute. She alright. But she's dope. The kind of woman who don't need to talk loud to get folks to listen. Moves like she owns her space. Got that clean, put-together look; blouse tucked crisp, bun neat, nails short and painted soft pink. Smelled faintly like vanilla and grape juice, a strange mix that somehow worked.

If she got in my bed, I wouldn't push her out, but that ain't what this was. She was solid. Cool. The kind of woman that makes you step your game up without ever sayin' a word. She had that glow to herself. Was it sex appeal, self-awareness, a quiet confidence, or maybe all of the above. Either I liked it and I hadn't said a word to her yet.

She looked up from her computer, eyes calm but sharp. "Can I help you, sir?"

"I hope so," I said. "Private car service. I handle executive, medical, airport runs, whatever y'all need."

She gave a slow nod. Looked me over. Not in a flirtatious way, in that "let me see what kind of man I'm dealin' with" kind of way.

Then she picked up my card, read it out loud, word for word. "Legacy Executive Transportation Services. L.E.T.S.; I like that." Her voice had this soft steadiness to it, like she'd been practicin' calm for years.

Then she tilted her head and said, "You got a picture?"

"A picture?" I said, blinkin'. "What in the hell do you need my picture for?" I said in my head.

Before I could even ask, she raised her phone. "Smile."

Click.

Didn't ask permission. Didn't overexplain. Just took it.

And that was that.

A week later, my phone rings. "Hey, this is Kirby Medical. We have a visiting surgeon coming in. You available?"

I said, "Yes ma'am, I am."

That was the first one. Then another. Then more. Every call came from her.

She never said much, just, "Pickup at Hobby. Passenger: Dr. Singh. Drop-off to Kirby." Or, "Patient transfer from Methodist to Memorial. Need discretion." And I'd say, "Always."

But after a while, we started talkin'. Not much. Just little things.

"How's business?" she'd ask.

"Busy enough to buy gas twice," I'd tell her.

She'd laugh. That kind of easy, unbothered laugh that could make a cloudy day back up and apologize. Sounded like peace.

Sometimes I'd swing by the office just to drop off new rate sheets. She'd be there, same calm energy, like the world couldn't shake her. Never flirty. Never fake. Just steady. And every now and then, I'd catch her watchin' me leave. Not long. Just a glance. Enough to let me know she saw me.

Then came the rain.

One gray afternoon she called for herself. Said she needed a ride downtown for a conference. Her voice had a little drag in it. Tired.

I pulled up front and she climbed in, holding a tote bag and a coffee that looked like she'd already forgotten she had. She sat down, let out a breath that sounded like she'd been holdin' it all week.

"Everybody needs me for somethin'," she said. "But they call it help."

I looked at her in the mirror. "Oh, you're a driver too."

She giggled. "Figures. You the driver. You see everybody else."

We rode in silence after that. The good kind. The kind where nobody feels the need to fill it.

Rain came steady, tapping the glass like quiet fingers. Wipers slid side to side. The city lights smeared across the windshield, stretched out like streaks of melted gold. She just stared out, face calm but far away.

About halfway there, she asked, "You ever get tired of takin' people where they wanna go when you don't even know where you're headed?" I laughed, but there wasn't any humor in it. "No," I said. "Right now, I get paid for my services. They get in, and I take them where they need to go, fair exchange. One day it will be my turn to sit back there, but I will know how the person who's driving feels and I will do right by them."

She nodded slow. "That's fair."

That was her, few words, heavy meaning. The kind that stick to you long after the car goes quiet.

When we got to the hotel, she lingered a second before openin' the door. "Thank you," she said. "For drivin'."

I said, "That's what I do."

She looked right at me. "No. For listenin'."

Then she was gone, walkin' into the rain with that same quiet confidence.

Next few months, she kept my phone buzzin'. Always business, always polite. Some people talk too much and give you nothin'. She could say two sentences and give you everything.

Every time her name popped up, I smiled a little. Not 'cause I wanted her, but because she reminded me that good energy still existed in the world, calm, decent, steady people just tryin' to move right; trying to get shit right in this crazy world we live in.

Then one morning, she called. Voice softer than usual.

"Hey," she said. "My great-aunt passed. Left me a house in Louisiana. I gotta head down there, handle things for a while."

I told her I was sorry. She thanked me, said she'd be back once it settled.

And that was it.

Maybe a month later, I dropped a client off at that clinic, she was gone. New girl at the desk. Same bowl of peppermints. Different vibe.

I asked what happened to the other lady.

"She moved," the girl said. "Family stuff."

I nodded and left. Didn't think much more about it.

Couple weeks later, I'm sittin' in the truck, half-eatin' a sandwich, scrollin' the news. Headline: Gas leak destroys home in small Louisiana town. One fatality.

I scrolled past it. Then I saw the update. They posted a picture.

Not the one I had, not the one she texted me from that company event with the champagne and that easy smile. This was older, stiffer. But I knew those eyes. That calm.

The sandwich sat in my lap gettin' cold. Didn't cry. Didn't call nobody. Just stared. Like maybe if I sat still enough, the truth would undo itself.

And all I could hear was her voice sayin', "You see everybody else."

I turned off the engine and just sat there. Rain had stopped but the air still smelled wet. I thought about that first day, her snappin' that damn picture like she already knew the ending. I scrolled to her name in my phone. Didn't text. Didn't delete. Just looked at it. It felt wrong to erase somebody who'd seen me that clearly.

After that, I couldn't bring myself to take her number out of my contacts. Every few months I clean my list, delete old clients, move the regulars into folders. But when I hit her name, I always skipped it.

Didn't matter that she was gone. She still had a place in my phone. In my head.

Sometimes, on slow nights, I'd scroll back through our old messages. Simple stuff. "Thank you." "Appreciate you." "Be safe."

Funny how normal words start soundin' sacred once the voice behind 'em goes quiet.

A few months later, I drove a doctor from that same clinic. Older guy. Kind face. He got in and asked, "You ever drive for us before?"

"Used to," I said. "More when Michelle was in the office."

He smiled. "Oh, you knew Michelle? He said, "Good woman. Always handled things right. Something was special about her, tragic loss." Then he got quiet. That silence told me he knew too.

We didn't talk the rest of the ride.

That night, I pulled over before goin' home. Sat there a long while, engine hummin', streetlights stretchin' long shadows across the dash. Thought about all the people who passed through my car, the loud, the lost, the lonely. And how every once in a while, somebody like Michelle slips in, steady and sure, and reminds you that there's still goodness left in the world.

She didn't owe me nothin'. Didn't flirt. Didn't promise. She just saw me. And sometimes, that's enough to keep you goin' when belief runs thin.

So here's to the ones who help you get in the door, even if they never walk through it with you. To the ones who see you before you see yourself. To the ones who make hard days feel lighter without even tryin'.

People talk about angels like they come with wings. But most of the ones I meet just wear scrubs, hold clipboards, or smile behind reception desks. They don't fly. They just show up. And then they disappear before you get the words out right.

If you ever met somebody like that, you know exactly what I mean. And if you haven't, maybe you already did. You just didn't realize it 'til they were gone.

SIX

THE LAWYERS

I met John Johnson Esq on one of those slow nights when I was just tryin' to fill the gaps. Hell, I don't even know why I said "extra money." I ain't never seen money that was extra. Every cent already had a job before it hit my hand.

It was a Wednesday, early fall, and the evening felt brisk compared to the heat of the day. I'd been drivin' all day, thinkin' about callin' it, but the ping came through: "Pickup, 62 E. Shore Drive, The Woodlands, TX." That's how I met him.

John Johnson Esq. Short, stocky, always in athletic gear with an Astros cap and this stringy hair peeking out the sides. Why you lookin' like that? Yeah, I know. You thought he was a brother huh? Everybody do. That name fools folks every time.

I even asked him once if he bought his name on eBay. He laughed so hard he snorted and said, "You know what, I might have!" We joked about it for a week after that. What made it funnier was I got a cousin with the same damn name, and they are nothing alike.

First time I drove him was to a Rockets game. He was the kinda guy who talked like he'd known you for years five minutes after meetin' you. Told me he liked how I moved. Said most drivers made him feel like a passenger. I told him, "That's because they drivin' for tips. I drive for respect." He laughed. Said that line alone was worth a twenty.

Next thing I know, I'm doin' airport runs, dinner parties, quick meetings, early morning courthouse drops. He kept callin'. And I kept answerin'.

That was my mistake. See, once you start gettin' too close to people that pay you, they start to treat you like they own you. You start to live in the space of obligation. John was married to Angela Torres Esq, and let me tell you, she was stunning. Long curly dark-brown hair, green-gray eyes, and a body that would stop time. Hell yes, I looked. My eyes work just fine. But it wasn't just how she looked; it was how she carried herself. Graceful, sharp, could hold her own in a room full of sharks and still smile without losin' her bite. Whew. Let me take a sip. Alright, enough about her. Damn she was fine though.

We met when I picked them up for a gala. She slid into the back seat and said, "You must be the famous driver my husband keeps talkin' about." I said, "I don't know about famous, ma'am, but I do stay booked." She smiled. "Booked is better than broke." From that moment, I liked her energy. She was kind, but not soft. Balanced.

I met their kids, their parents, their staff, everybody. Whole family treated me like one of their own. That part felt good. They weren't my usual kind of rich clients. They had new money, the kind that still squeaks when it moves. Still excited to show it off. Still actin' surprised that they had it.

He once told me, "Man, I just bought a yacht you're gonna love, but I had to buy a house so I'd have somewhere to store it." I said, "You mean a boathouse?" He said, "No, a house-house." And I'm like, "Wait, what?" He said, "Yeah, I literally parked the boat in the house. In the garage. Had to get a custom door put in and everything." I just nodded, sittin' there thinkin' about my seven-hundred-square-foot apartment and the way my rent kept climbin' like it was tryin' to join the clouds.

Different worlds. But I was genuinely happy for him. One day he calls me to Top Golf. Said he wanted to bring me in as a "travel liaison" for his firm. Told me I'd get medical benefits, an office, business cards with my name in shiny embossed silver print. Sprinter van, box seats, the works. Sounded good. But I figured, hell, if you stand next to success long enough, maybe some of it rubs off. Plus, I really liked him. I treated him like a friend.

So I took the job.

For a few months, I was eatin'. Calendar stayed full, checks hittin' on time. Not much, but it was consistent money. Had a company laptop, a dark little office, keys to the house and all of the vehicles. There I go again with that "extra-money" talk. Smh. Then came the Austin trip. He wanted me to drive him and Angela for a weekend getaway, leave Friday, come back Monday night. Sounded simple enough. But when I started runnin' the numbers, I realized I was makin' less money now than before this "arrangement." Between the flat salary, the gas, and the overtime he kept callin' "the cost of opportunity," I was basically payin' myself to drive him. I had already committed so I went.

We hit 290 that Friday evenin'. The city fell away behind us, all lights and noise, and the road stretched long and quiet. Angela was in the back, half asleep against the window, earbuds in. John was on the phone the whole time, talkin' big, laughin' louder, droppin' phrases like "liquid assets" and "client leverage" like confetti. I just drove, music low, watchin' the horizon melt orange into black.

Halfway there, he muted his call, leaned up, and said, "You know, you're lucky to be workin' with me. Most people never get this close to real power." I said, "Maybe. But power and peace don't always live in the same house." He smiled like he didn't hear me, then went right back to talkin' numbers.

When we pulled up to the Austin house, Angela thanked me like she always did. John didn't. He tossed me the keys to the private quarters, said, "See you in the morning." It was somethin' in that simple act that burnt a fire inside of me. I felt it, that shift from client to owner. From respect to control.

The next two days were quiet on the outside but loud in my head. They argued a little in the kitchen once, not loud, but sharp. Sunday night, I saw Angela sittin' outside by herself, phone glowin' against her face, eyes wet. I wanted to ask if she was alright, but that's not my lane. I drive. I don't interfere. Still, I saw it. And I remembered.

By the time we rolled back into Houston Monday night, I knew I was done. Over the next few weeks, John started changin'. Got sharper with his words, colder with his tone. Talked about people like they were pawns.

"People will always need me before I need them," he told me once. Said it like scripture. He'd brag about winnin' cases and destroyin' people's lives like it was sport. Called his partners every name in the book behind their backs. People he smiled with in court, shook hands with at events, he'd tear them apart the second they left the room.

That kind of energy leaves residue. You can feel it even when he's laughin'. The air gets thick. And I started wonderin' how long before he turned that same sharpness my way.

Then came the night that told me everything I needed to know.

He called me out the blue around nine. Said he needed a quick ride to Midtown. I picked him up at his house, Angela's car was gone.

He was grinnin', smellin' like a bad mix of cologne and curry. Horrible combination, but hey, to each their own. We pulled up to a nice apartment complex, valet lights glowin' soft. He said, "Keep the car runnin'. I'll be ten minutes." *Keep the car runnin'*, he said. This ain't even his damn car, I thought. Ten turned to thirty. Thirty turned to forty-five. When he came out, shirt half-tucked, smile crooked, he slid in and said, "That's Rodriguez's girl. Kid don't even know." Then he laughed. Said somethin' about "leverage workin' in more ways than one."

I didn't laugh. Didn't even look at him. Just drove. But in my head, I was already done. I just didn't know how to say it yet. It was right then I knew, that motherfucker don't respect nobody. Not his partners. Not his associates. Not Rodriguez. Not even me. I'm just the driver who's supposed to pretend I didn't see shit.

Nah. I saw it. And I remembered. See, if a man'll cheat on his wife, especially with an associate's wife or girlfriend, he'll fuck you over in time too. The new golden rule: Don't let nobody fuck you unless you wanna get fucked. And that works in more ways than one.

Anyway, he told me to take him to Austin the upcoming weekend. No more *Are you available this night?* What do you think of this? He started to demand. And that was it. I told them we needed to revisit our agreement. We met in his office, glass walls, fancy desk, trophies on every shelf. I sat across from him and said it plain.

"John, I appreciate the opportunity, but the numbers don't add up. Legacy's what's underperforming, not me. If you want me gone seventy-plus hours, it's sixty-five an hour minimum, and that's the cheapest rate you'll find."

He leaned back, smilin' that fake calm. Said, "You're startin' to sound ungrateful." I said, "Nah, you got me fucked up. I appreciate the experience but don't be confused by my kindness."

He didn't like that.

He then said that the firm is doin' some restructuring and my services were no longer needed. Said it wasn't personal, just business. Asked me to return the keys to his house, his vehicles, the laptop. Spoke like he was firing an employee.

I said, "John, you run a law firm, but you don't run me. There's a difference between a client and an employee. You were a client. Clients don't fire vendors. They just stop gettin' serviced. And I already stopped servin' you the moment I walked into this office. So nah, you didn't fire me. I been quit. You just didn't know it yet."

He blinked, lips tight, trying not to show it got under his skin. I handed him his keys, laptop, and walked out. Never looked back.

That night, I had a different client. I thought about how different he was compared to John. How much more regal he was, reserved. People come from all walks of life. And I realized something. The law might protect property, but it don't always protect people. Sometimes the folks writin' the rules are the same ones breakin' them, just with better pens.

John Johnson Esq taught me more than any book could. He taught me that money don't buy class. That power without character is poison. And that silence, sometimes, is what they pay for most.

See, people like him keep drivers like me close for a reason. We see everything. We hear everything. We know who they really are when the ties come off and the liquor kicks in. We become their confessional. Their witness. Their alibi if things go bad.

But here's the truth they forget: Some of us got memories sharper than their contracts.

A few months after that, I saw him again, purely by accident. I was parked outside a restaurant in River Oaks waitin' on a pickup. He walked out with a group of men, laughin', cigar hangin' from his mouth. He saw me, froze a second, then raised his glass like a toast. I nodded back, not outta respect, just recognition. He'll always remember that I know somethin' he hopes nobody ever finds out.

Funny thing about power: it's only power if people believe in it. Once they stop believin', it's just noise.

As I listen to myself tell you the story now, I realize there are two kinds of rich folks, the ones who pay for convenience, and the ones who pay for control. He was the second kind. And I promised myself I'd never be the type of man who made another man feel small just to feel big. I pulled out my phone, updated my client list, deleted his number. Felt good. Clean. Freedom smells like fresh tires and a full tank.

As I sat there, I thought about all the people I'd driven since I started—CEOs, pastors, rappers, newlyweds, liars, cheaters, dreamers. Every one of them taught me somethin'. But the lawyers? They taught me the fine print of human nature. That integrity don't come with a degree. And that silence is worth more than retainer fees.

With that said, here's to knowin' when somebody's playin' you. And knowin' when to walk the fuck away.

SEVEN

THE SILENT PASSENGER

Now you done got my blood pressure up talkin' about that idiot. Let me relax my nerves a bit.

Did you eat yet? Thirsty? Ok, I'm just checkin'. I don't want you lookin' at me crazy and goin' around tellin' everybody that this dude wouldn't shut the fuck up and I was about to pass out.

Ok, I'm back. Man. I still don't know what to make of this shit.

I been drivin' long enough to have seen some shit, trust me. But this? This was different.

Let me pour another drink first. OK.

I should've been home hours ago.

It'd been one of those nights, three airport runs, a bachelor party that tipped in singles like I was a damn stripper, and a couple who fought the whole way to their hotel and then asked me to wait while they "worked it out."

I didn't wait.

By the time I got back to Bush, it was past 2 a.m. and I was ready to call it. My back hurt. My eyes were dry. I had that weird headache you get when you've been starin' at taillights too long.

But then the app pinged.

Terminal C. The Woodlands. Eighty-five bucks.

I thought about ignorin' it. Thought about turnin' the app off and goin' home. But eighty-five dollars is eighty-five dollars.

And I told myself, "One more. Just one more and you're done."

Famous last words.

It's around three in the mornin'. That strange hour when time don't make sense and the city sound asleep but you still movin'.

I'm parked at Bush Airport, waitin' zone, scrollin' through my phone, halfway through a bag of Flamin' Hots. I probably shouldn't be eatin' that late, the way my acid reflux is set up.

I get an alert that the flight has landed. Easy run. Pickup: Terminal C. Drop-off: The Woodlands.

Forty-minute ride. Eighty-five dollars easy. Take that, Airline.

I toss the chips, wipe my hands, and pull around.

Terminal C stay quiet at that hour. No crowd, just stragglers, folks comin' in on them last flights from wherever people fly in from at 3 a.m.

I pull up, pop the trunk, and wait.

Then I see him.

White dude. Maybe forty, maybe fifty. Hard to tell. Average

height, average build, average everything. Brown jacket, jeans, one of them black roller bags, the kind everybody got.

Nothin' about him stood out. If I passed him on the street, I wouldn't remember his face five seconds later.

But somethin' about the way he moved felt... off.

Not fast. Not slow. Just... mechanical. Like he was goin' through motions he'd done a thousand times but didn't remember doin'.

He didn't look around. Didn't check his phone. Just walked straight toward my truck like he already knew which one was mine.

And when he got close, I noticed somethin' else.

No expression. Not tired. Not stressed. Not relieved to finally be gettin' a ride.

Just... blank. Like a mannequin someone had programmed to walk.

He walks up, nods, barely, and tosses his bag in the trunk.

I heard it land. Heard the thud. Felt the truck dip just slightly from the weight. I remember thinkin', that's a heavy bag for a carry-on.

Then he climbed in the back without a word.

I say, "How you doin' tonight?"

Nothin'.

I glance in the rearview. He's sittin' there starin' out the window.

Aight. Quiet type. I get it. Not everybody wanna talk at 3 a.m. I respect that.

I pull off.

Now I'm used to silence. Some of my best rides been quiet. But this wasn't that peaceful kind. This was heavy. Like the air itself got weight on it.

Hardy Toll Road stretched out empty and black. No other cars. No streetlights for long stretches. Just me, the hum of the tires, and the glow from the dash.

I turned the radio on. Old R&B station. Quiet Storm hour. Anita Baker, Luther Vandross, the kind of slow songs that usually make a drive feel smooth.

But tonight it felt wrong. Like the music was tryin' too hard to fill a space that didn't wanna be filled.

I glanced in the rearview again. He was still starin' out the window. Hadn't moved. Hadn't shifted. Hadn't even blinked as far as I could tell.

And that's when I noticed somethin' else.

He wasn't lookin' at anything.

We passed signs, overpasses, the glow of a 24-hour gas station in the distance and his eyes never tracked any of it. Just stared. Like he was lookin' through the window instead of out of it.

I try again. "First time in Houston?"

Nothin'. Not even a grunt.

Just that stare.

And that shit was creepin' me out. I didn't stay out past midnight just to ride with some weirdo.

I check the mirror again. He ain't on his phone, no earbuds, no nothin'.

Just sittin'. Like a mannequin.

My hands started to sweat. I told myself I was bein' ridiculous. Dude's probably just tired. Probably had a long flight. Probably doesn't feel like talkin' to a stranger at 3 in the morning.

But my body wasn't listenin' to my brain.

My chest felt tight. My breathing got shallow. That tightness in your gut when somethin' don't sit right, that's what I had.

I wanted to say somethin'. Anything. Just to break the silence.

But every time I opened my mouth, the words died before they got out.

Like the air itself was tellin' me, Don't.

So I turn the music down low and just drive.

I-45 was empty, which is weird since there's always something happening on 45. Just me, the hum of the tires, the glow from the dash.

Peaceful in theory. But that quiet started crawlin' up my neck.

I kept glancin' back every few minutes just to make sure dude was still alive. I definitely don't wanna be ridin' around with some dead dude in the back seat. Don't people shit and piss when they die? I thought. Hell naw, I don't wanna deal with that.

Every time, same thing. Stiff. Still. Starin'. Barely blinkin'.

About twenty minutes in, I tried one more time.

"You visitin' family? Business?"

Nothin'. Not even a head turn.

I looked at him in the mirror, and for just a second, just a flash, I thought I saw him blink.

But I wasn't sure.

And that made it worse.

We ride like that thirty, maybe forty minutes. Not a word. Not a cough. Not even a breath I could hear.

By the time we hit The Woodlands, I can feel that wrong energy fillin' the car. You ever get that tightness in your chest like your body know somethin' before your brain do? That.

Finally, I pull up to the address. Nice house. Two-story. Big yard. All lights off. Quiet neighborhood.

I put it in park and say, "Aight, we here."

Dude don't say nothin'. Just opens the door, steps out, and walks toward the house.

Cool. Whatever. Let me grab his bag.

I pop the trunk. Walk around back.

And stop.

The trunk's empty.

I blink. Look again. Still empty.

I run my hand along the carpet, like maybe the bag slid to the side or somehow got wedged in a corner.

Nothin'.

My heart starts poundin'. I know I heard it. I felt the truck dip when he put it in. I watched him do it. Didn't I?

I pull out my phone, check the booking. One passenger. One bag.

I look back at the house. Still dark. No porch light. No movement. No sign that anyone even went inside.

I walk up to the front door. Slow. Quiet.

I don't knock. I just stand there, listenin'.

Nothin'. No footsteps. No TV. No voices.

Just silence.

I circle around to the side of the house, peekin' through the fence. No lights on in the back either. No car in the driveway.

It's like the house is... empty. Like nobody lives there at all.

Now I'm standin' there, starin' at this house like a damn fool. Tryin' to make sense of it.

I go back to the truck, slow, like I'm expectin' somebody to jump out and yell "Gotcha!"

Nothin'.

I sit in the driver's seat, look at the payment processor. Trip complete. Payment processed.

Eighty-five dollars.

The ride's real. But where the hell did dude go? The bag?

I look in the backseat. Empty.

I know I'm not trippin'. Thirty minutes of silence.

Am I?

Now I'm sittin' there, starin' at my own reflection in the mirror, wonderin' if I just lost it.

Did I drive somebody? Or did I just drive myself through the dark talkin' to nobody?

I think about callin' my brother. My cousin.

Damn, what I'm supposed to say? "Hey man, this motherfucker just vanished"?

So I don't call.

I just sit there. Wait.

House stay dark. No movement. No light.

After a while I put it in drive and roll off slow. Like leavin' a graveyard.

The whole ride back I keep replayin' it.

The pickup. The trunk. The stare. The silence.

Every part feels real. But every time I think about his face, it's gone. Blank.

Like somebody took an eraser to my memory.

I park back at my apartment. Engine off. Lights off. Just sittin'.

I go inside. Pour a drink. Then another.

Sit on the couch and stare at the wall.

I tried to think. Tried to remember his face.

But every time I reached for it, it slipped away. Like tryin' to grab smoke.

I remembered the jacket. The jeans. The bag.

But his face? Gone.

I pulled up the app, looked at the ride details.

Pickup time: 3:14 a.m. Drop-off time: 3:52 a.m. Route tracked. Payment processed.

Everything logged.

So it happened. Right?

I drove someone. They paid. They got out.

But then where'd the bag go? And where'd he go?

A week later, I'm drivin' someone else to The Woodlands. Different address. Different passenger. Completely normal ride.

But when we turned onto Hardy Toll Road, my hands started shakin'.

I kept checkin' the rearview. Kept waitin' for my passenger to go silent. To stare out the window like he did.

They didn't. They were on their phone, scrollin', completely normal.

But I couldn't shake it.

When I dropped them off, I sat in the car for ten minutes before drivin' away. Just to make sure they were real. Just to make sure I saw them walk inside.

And that's when I realized: It wasn't about whether he was real. It was about whether I could trust what I saw anymore.

Ever since that night, I check the backseat twice. Before and after every ride.

If they got a bag, I make sure it's still there when they leave.

You probably think I'm crazy. Maybe I am.

But that night happened.

Maybe it was a glitch in the system. Maybe I drove somebody who wasn't supposed to be picked up yet. Or maybe they already been dropped off. Somewhere else.

I don't know.

All I know is I got paid for it. And I can't refund money to somebody who don't exist.

So I kept it. And I kept drivin'.

Sometimes, late at night, on them empty stretches of road, I think about that man. Starin' out the window. Sayin' nothin'. Goin' nowhere.

EIGHT
THE BACHELOR PARTY

L et me tell you about the time I had a bachelor party pickup. Man... it never seem to amaze me at the things people do just before they get married. I had a pickup at The Core Apartments, right across from Buffalo Wild Wings and Five Guys over on Washington in the Heights. Soon as I pull up, I already know it's gonna be a long night. Music bumpin', doors swingin', folks laughin' too loud, liquor smell before they even hit the curb. They climb in like clowns in a circus, talkin' loud, spillin' drinks, actin' like the night had already ended and they needed to take their asses to bed. One of 'em leans over my shoulder and yells, "Ayy yo, driver, we good to roll!" No doubt, I said, matching their energy. I count six in the mirror. The groom, best man, two partners, and two women they swear "wasn't supposed to be there." Not my business. My job is simple. Drive. Stay out the way. Bring they asses back home. Simple. Where to? I asked. "Downtown first," the best man says. I hit the lights and ease into traffic.

On the way, the groom's phone won't stop buzzin'. He keeps flippin' it over like that will stop whoever is calling. The best man got a bottle open and already passin' it around. Somebody tries to hand it to me. "I'm good'," I say. "You sure?" he says. "I'm sure. I don't drink" (wink)

We pull up to a spot off Main. I ain't namin' it. If you from Houston, you know the type. Valets hustlin', door line movin', bass rattlin' the sidewalk. Security do that head nod like they running shit. You know, a typical night out. All was missing was a dude taking pictures with a backdrop. Do they still do that shit?

The crew spills out and disappears inside like they got swallowed. I stay put. AC on low, eyes on the door. I scroll a little, look up a lot. Nothing out of the ordinary..

An hour goes by. Then a little more. The door opens and the night walks out again. Best man got the groom under his arm like a busted suitcase. One partner mad for no reason. The other tryin' to calm everybody down while starin' at his phone like he wished she would call, but she's not. One of the women cussin' at some guy that she said grabbed her ass, but she don't have no ass to grab. Maybe she should've said he rubbed against her back. Yeah, that's it, because that's all she had. The other got that tired smile that ain't happy, that i'm done and ready to go home look.

They tumble into the truck, still talking about the events or lack thereof in the club. "We hittin' Richmond," best man says. "You sure?" I ask. "We celebratin', baby," he says. "No doubt! let's do it!"

We hit a spot on Richmond. Same rules, different music.

I stay in the truck. Windows cracked. Nothing on the radio. Twenty minutes later, one of the women comes back out and sits up front with me. Hands in her lap, phone face down. "You good?" I ask. "I'm tired of babysittin' grown men," she says. "Oh, you a driver too?" I say. She laughs at that. Real little laugh. No flirtin'. Just two tired people sharin' the same air.

We sit quiet after that. People-watchin'. Door swings, bodies pass, night rolls on.

Half an hour later, the groom comes out with somebody that wasn't with us. Tall. Attractive. Red dress. He has his hand on her lower back like he forgot there's a world out here. She moves steady. Sober. Not messy. Just... steady. But I ain't gonna lie, somethin' about her didn't line up. Not wrong. Just off. Can't even name it. And I don't try to. I don't stare. I clock it, then let it go.

They go back in. Best man disappears again and pop up again like his ass is The Great Gazoo. Closing time hits and the door throws everybody back to the street. Security escorts two of mine like luggage. One got a split lip. The other got that drunk chest-out tough talk. The woman from my front seat shakes her head like she predicted all of it.

The groom is last out, holdin' hands with red dress. He looks like he lost and found himself twice tonight. "Back to The Core," best man says through his teeth. "Y'all good?" I ask. "We great," he lies.

We roll. The vibe is not the same. They quiet as hell. These motherfuckers done had it. The woman up front leans her head against the glass with her eyes closed. The red dress woman sits quiet. Groom leans forward and whispers like secrets ain't got volume.

"You ever feel like you ain't built for what people want from you?" he says. "You drunk," I say. "That ain't a feelin'. That's a forecast." He huffs, then sits back.

We stop at The Core first. Best man fumbles cash, tries to tip me with funny money. I hold it to the dome light and say no you can keep that shit. He finds the real roll and hands it over like it's hurting him to part with it. Some people want it all, first class all they way but when it's time to pay, they forget what money is. Not on my watch The two partners stumble inside. The woman from the front seat squeezes my shoulder and says thanks, then walks in barefoot, heels in her hand. Head steady.

The groom stands on the curb, lookin' like a decision he don't wanna make. "You takin' her home?" he asks, chin toward red dress. "If she needs a ride," I say. Red dress nods. "Montrose," she says. "Off Westheimer." I know the area.

Best man tugs on the groom's sleeve. "Come on." "I'm good," the groom says. "Y'all go. I'm good, I'll meet you inside" They go. He don't.

We pull off. Me and red dress. She looks out the window. Bag in her lap. Calm like she practiced. Up close, I see it more clear. Features soft and sharp in the same place. Makeup clean. Voice low when she answers simple questions. And again, somethin' else I clocked but didn't name. No judgment. Just a note my brain wrote and put away.

"You good?" I ask. "I'm fine," she says. "But thank you for askin'." We ride in that good quiet. No radio. No small talk.

Near her block she says, "You can let me out by that corner." "You sure?" I ask. "I'm sure," she says with uncertainty.

I put it in park. She takes out flats, slides them on like her feet been prayin' for them. She folds a couple bills and tucks it in the cup holder. "For bein' decent," she says. "We all desire love. That shows up differently for everybody," I say. She nods, steps out, closes the door soft, and heads down the sidewalk with purpose.

I pull off and go to taco truck down the street in the Valero gas station parking lot. I park across the street and just sit a minute to collect my thoughts. I turn off the radio, and let silence be the song. I'm thinkin' about how fast a night can teach a man who he is and who he ain't.

Then I see him. The groom. How this motherfucker get over here? On the sidewalk by the truck. Shirt open, hair messed, walkin' crooked, on the phone, alone.

Then I spot the red dress walking up. He calls her name. She looks him up and down like she got scales in her eyes. He says somethin' I can't hear. She tilts her head. He steps close. Puts a hand on her arm. She doesn't flinch. He leans in and kisses her. Not nasty. Not sloppy. Just... soft. Like he finally remembered how to be a person, not a mascot.

She lets him, then settles him back with a hand on his chest. Says somethin' low. Then she looks past him. At me. Not the truck. Me. Like she knew I'd still be around.

I try not to judge, but I know this guy is about to get married and she's definitely not the bride. We all have our skeletons, I think, just clean your closet before you let someone hang up their clothes.

I breathe in slow. The city breathes with me.

And that's when I see him again. He's standing there, hands on his head, talking to himself like he's arguing with God. He drops to the curb, elbows on knees, phone in his hand but not calling nobody. He's shaking his head like he finally ran out of lies to tell himself. The red dress woman's gone, vanished into the night like she was never there, and he's just sitting there under the yellow streetlight looking small.

I watch a long time. Too long maybe. He tries to light a cigarette, drops it, tries again. Hands trembling. He looks up like he wants the sky to answer something. I know that look. That's the look of a man who just realized the party wasn't the celebration, it was the cover. He's breaking quiet. That soft kind of breakdown that don't need witnesses but still begs for one.

He wipes his face, maybe from sweat, maybe tears. I can't tell. I somehow feel his pain. Not from judgement. From recognition. I've been there too. Different place, different circumstance, but same hurt nonetheless. Then he stands, straightens his shirt, and for a second I see it, the man he wants to be fighting to crawl back through the wreckage. He don't win, not yet, but he's trying.

I could've called out. Could've told him it's okay, or that nobody's built for everything people expect from them. But I've learned the road don't need commentary, it needs distance. So I let him have his silence. Sometimes silence is the mercy. They ain't doin' nothin' but talkin' now, him and that night. I can see it in the slump of his shoulders. He's listening to whatever truth finally caught up. I couldn't let ole boy walk back home or however he got to that taco truck, so I go and get me a taco, offer him one and a bottle water and a ride home. It's time to go home buddy. Get some rest. I say. We head back to The Core. I text the best man: "Your boy's safe. Handle your side." He texts back, "You gettin' extra for this." I text, "No worries"

I park where I started. Engine on. Window cracked. Night air heavy. I look at my hands. I think about brides and grooms and secrets and lies, and the little pockets of quiet where folks try to figure out who they are without the whole world lookin'.

The next afternoon my phone lights up from an unknown number. "Thank you for last night. For the ride. For the quiet."

No name. Just a taco emoji. I laugh so hard I put the phone down.

A few days later the groom books me for an early airport run. He gets in the back, clear-eyed, no show. Halfway down 59 he says, "We good?" "Always, you?" I say. "I am," he says.

We don't talk after that.

At Departures he hands me an envelope. No speech. Just that quick pass men do when they ain't got the words. It's thick. I put it in my armrest.

As he got out of the car, I watch a woman meet him at the curb and hug him like she knows what happened and decided it don't change nothin'. It was somber, slow motion, but soothing somehow. He keeps his head down different now. Not shame. Maybe respect. Maybe tired. They walk in together holding hands.

And that's when it hits me. Secrets ain't always poison. Sometimes they're just pain that never found a safe place to sit. Grace is when somebody sees it and don't flinch. When they look at your mess and still choose to stay kind. Maybe that's what red dress was, grace in heels. Maybe that's what I was too for a few hours. A man giving somebody's guilt a quiet ride home.

I ain't the judge of nobody's life at three in the morning. What I saw wasn't a scandal. It was a mess. A human one. A quiet corner where a man kissed a woman who already knew more about him than he knows about himself.

To the wild nights that don't need a weekend. To the people learnin' who they are in public.

NINE
MR. DAVID'S SON

Back in the late 90s, Houston didn't feel like a big city yet. You could still hear the hum of crickets at night if you turned the radio down and cracked the window. Folks said good morning like they meant it, not because it was polite but because it was part of who they were. There was a softness to the city then, before the cranes, before the sprawl, before the traffic turned every freeway into a waiting room. Before Katrina brought a different kind of storm, not wind and rain, but people. Families, souls, whole communities from places that got hit hard. They came looking for new beginnings, and Houston opened its arms. The skyline didn't change that year, but the feel of the city did.

That Houston had charm, old-school, slow, and warm. The kind of place where barbers knew your daddy's middle name and everybody waved from their porch just because. People took pride in being from Houston, but it still carried the heart of a small town. Everybody knew somebody who knew somebody. And for us, that somebody was Mr. David.

Mr. David was one of my father's longtime clients, sharp mind, sharper dresser. Not old money, but earned money. He built his name the hard way, through years in courtrooms and long nights reading law books under bad lighting. He came from a line of strength, descendants of the very people in Galveston who didn't know they were free until long after freedom had been signed into law. The same people whose delayed liberation gave birth to Juneteenth. Every success he had carried that legacy with it. You could see it in the way he walked, quiet pride, hard-won dignity.

One afternoon, Mr. David introduced me to his son. He said, "Jr., this is Mr. Otis's son," then added my name like a footnote.

The boy couldn't have been more than seven or eight. Straight-backed, well-mannered, a little man in miniature. But when he heard Mr. Otis's son, something about it stuck. He stepped forward, extended his hand, and said in the clearest little voice, "Hello, Mr. Otis Son."

I remember looking down at him, trying not to laugh. He had that serious look children get when they're trying to prove they belong in grown-folk spaces. I shook his hand and said, "Pleasure to meet you, Mr. David's son."

He froze for half a second, then his face softened into a grin. "I like that," he said.

From that day on, that's what we were to each other. Mr. Otis's son and Mr. David's son. Titles earned through respect and rhythm.

He was different from other kids. While most were glued to Game Boys or bouncing in their seats, he'd sit back and unfold a USA Today like it was the morning brief. Page after page, eyes scanning headlines about politics and markets he couldn't possibly understand yet. He read that paper religiously. And then, just when I'd think he was lost in adult business, he'd drop a question that reminded you he was still a kid, curious, wild, and full of wonder.

"Why do some people say the man on the moon and some people say the man in the moon? Which one is it?" Or, "What's Wed-ness and why does it get a day?"

He stretched words apart just to see what they sounded like. Wanted to know why people said things the way they did, what words meant underneath what they meant. I used to think he'd grow out of it, that he'd turn into one of those teenagers who thought they already knew everything. But even then, I could tell that boy's mind didn't have an off switch.

When I dropped him and his father off, he'd always turn around after getting out. "See you later, Mr. Otis Son." And I'd answer, "Take care, Mr. David's son."

That became our thing. The handshake, the banter, the small talk between two souls from different corners of life, bound by curiosity and respect.

About a year later, life pulled me away. My mother's health was slipping, and duty outweighed comfort. I packed up, left Houston, and went back to Chicago to care for her. The city welcomed me like an old friend, same cold wind, same grit, but part of me missed that Texas warmth. Missed the slow rhythm of life where people still looked each other in the eye. It felt different; I'd seen different, wanted different, deserved different.

Every now and then, my father would call me and mention the boy. "Mr. David's son asked about you again," he'd say. "Said to tell Mr. Otis's son hello."

I asked him once, "Did he actually say my name?" My father laughed. "No, son. Still Mr. Otis Son. He ain't letting that go."

That always made me smile. Kids forget names, but they remember how you made them feel.

Time moved, the way it does. My mother passed, and the silence after was heavier than any suitcase I'd carried. Grief makes you question everything, what matters, what doesn't, who you really are when the noise stops. For a while, I stayed put. Worked odd jobs, kept my head down. There were days when I'd hear a child laugh outside and swear it sounded like him. Memory plays tricks like that. The heart don't know how to let go, it just learns how to hum quieter.

After some time, I decided I needed a change of air, and Houston felt like the right place to breathe again.

When I moved back, my father was still driving. One morning my phone rang. It was him. "You want to pick up your buddy today?" he asked.

"My buddy?"

He chuckled. "Mr. David's boy. He's all grown up now. Big shot."

I didn't hesitate. "Yeah, I'll take that one."

When I pulled up to the house, the front door opened, and out stepped a man I almost didn't recognize. Tall, about six-four, built like he'd been created in Men's Health magazine. Perfect posture, calm confidence. But then he smiled, and I saw the same spark I remembered from the backseat of that limo.

"Mr. Otis Son!" he shouted, voice deeper but full of the same joy.

Before I could get a word out, he wrapped me in a hug that nearly cracked a damn rib. I laughed. "You can't be that little boy who used to read USA Today every ride."

He grinned. "Still do. Just on a tablet now."

We laughed the whole ride. He told me about school, internships, how he hustled his way into the corporate world. Said he learned early that curiosity was a muscle, and that asking questions most people ignored ended up being his superpower.

We hit traffic near Allen Parkway and just kept talking. He told me about his father, how Mr. David had passed a few years earlier, and how that changed him. "You spend your whole life trying to live up to somebody's name," he said, looking out the window, "then one day that name is yours to carry alone. It's heavier than I thought."

That line stayed with me. The truth in it. How the titles we inherit come with invisible weight. There's some shit men can't let go and that was one of them. I couldn't relate, but I truly understood.

When we reached his stop, he paused before getting out. "You know, I never forgot that," he said.

"Forgot what?" I asked.

"That day you called me Mr. David's son. Made me feel like I was somebody."

That's something else. Because I wasn't trying to teach him anything that day. I was just mirroring respect. But sometimes, what's small to you becomes sacred to somebody else.

We stayed in touch. Not every day, just enough to remind each other we were still out here, still pushing. Over the years, I'd see his name pop up: new job, new promotion, marriage, first child, then a second. I saw his TED Talk online one night. The topic was leadership, but underneath it all was the same voice of that boy asking was the man in or on the moon.

He said something in that talk that made me pause: "Sometimes the people who shape you the most, don't even know they did. They're just doing their work, showing you what humility looks like in motion."

He never said my name, but I didn't need him to. I knew.

Years later, he invited me to his father's memorial scholarship dinner. I almost didn't go, drivers get used to being invisible, but something told me to show up. When I walked in, he stopped mid-speech and pointed toward me. "That man right there taught me what legacy really means." Whole room turned. Cameras. Applause. I ain't built for spotlights, but that one moment felt like a circle closing.

Afterward, he shook my hand and whispered, "Still Mr. Otis Son to me." I nodded. "Always, Mr. David's son."

These days we don't talk often. Life has its pace, and success has its price. But every once in a while, my phone buzzes with a text that says, "Hey Mr. Otis Son." No reason. No follow-up. Just that.

And every time, I smile.

I'm proud of that young man. Proud that his curiosity paid off. Proud that I got to see the seed and the tree.

I don't drive limos anymore. Haven't for a while. These days I drive big rigs, cross-country hauls, long stretches of road where silence keeps you company better than any conversation could. The hum of those engines is my soundtrack now, and somewhere between mile markers I still replay that first handshake, that small boy voice calling me Mr. Otis Son.

Sometimes I pass through Houston again. I'll stop at a diner on 290 or a truck stop on 45, sip coffee out of a chipped mug, and watch the people move. Families. Fathers and sons. A man teaching his boy how to pump gas, another showing his kid how to fold a map even though the world runs on phones now. I see echoes of that bond everywhere.

Every so often, when the road is long and the sky is quiet, I think about how simple words can travel across decades. Mr. David's son. Mr. Otis's son. What started as a playful exchange turned into a reminder that what you call somebody can either shrink them or set them free.

I realize now it wasn't just about names, it was about acknowledgment. About seeing people, even the ones the world drives past.

Sometimes I think about what his father said that first day. "This is Mr. Otis's son."

It was meant to explain who I was, but to that boy, it became who I am. And that's fine by me. Because somewhere out there, a grown man who used to ask about Wed-ness Day and the man in the moon is making decisions that shape the world, and in the small, quiet way that only a driver knows, I got to be part of that journey.

And maybe that's what legacy really is, not fame, not wealth, just leaving a little bit of good behind in someone who carries it forward.

So when that text pings again and I see, Hey, Mr. Otis Son, I don't even need to answer. I just whisper back to the road, "Hey, Mr. David's son. Keep goin'."

TEN
THE COST OF FREEDOM

I t's been a whole chapter since we talked. I need to refresh my drink with this next story.

Now, you aren't telling nobody what we talked about, right? Don't have me come looking for you, telling these people business. This just between me and you. Nah, I'm serious. Some stories aren't mine to tell. They're mine to hold. Big difference.

But this one?

This one stays with me. Even now, years later, when I'm rolling through some lonely stretch of I-10 in the middle of the night, windows down, radio low, this story finds its way back to me. Makes me think about trust, about love, about the thousand ways people lie to themselves before they ever lie to someone else.

So pour yourself something strong. This one's long, and it's complicated, and it don't end the way you think it will.

His name was Marcus.

Tall brother, about six-two, clean-cut, the kind of man who looked like he had his life figured out. Corporate job, nice house in Katy, wore a wedding ring that caught the light every time he checked his watch. Which he did often. Too often.

First time I picked him up, I peeped him immediately. Dude seemed off, as my old pastor use to say "he had that far off look." Eyes darting. He wasn't checking emails on his phone. He was checking something, but it wasn't work. Every notification made his jaw tighten. Every buzz made him flinch.

I didn't say anything. That's the job. You watch, you listen, you drive. You don't ask questions unless they ask first.

But Marcus?

You can tell Marcus needed to talk. He just didn't know how to start.

We were halfway to his meeting when he finally broke.

"You ever been married?"

I glanced at him in the rearview. "Once."

"Still?"

"Nah."

He nodded slow, like I'd just confirmed something he already suspected about the world.

"How'd you know it was over?" he asked.

I could've told him the truth, that I didn't know until it already was. That sometimes the end happens so quiet you don't hear it coming. But I didn't think that's what he needed to hear.

"When the silence stops feeling comfortable," I said. "When you're in the same room and it feels like you're alone."

He stared out the window for a long time.

"Yeah," he said finally. "That's where I'm at."

Over the next few weeks, Marcus became a regular. Same time, same route, same haunted look in his eyes. And little by little, the story came out.

Her name was Diane. They'd been married nine years. High school sweethearts who beat the odds, or so everyone said. Two kids, both under eight. Good jobs, good neighborhood, good life.

Except something had shifted.

At first, it was small things. She started going to the gym more. New clothes. New hairstyles. New perfume. She'd laugh at her phone and then go quiet when he walked in the room. She stopped asking about his day. Stopped initiating anything. Not arguments, not conversations, not sex and rejected him on multiple occasions if he tried. Just stopped.

Marcus did what most men do when their gut tells them something's wrong but their pride won't let them ask.

He started looking.

"I checked her phone one night," he said, voice low, ashamed. "While she was in the shower."

I didn't say nothing. Just drove.

"Found messages," he continued. "But they weren't what I expected."

"What'd you expect?" I asked.

"Another man. You know, the usual. A work husband telling her shit I missed, some gym trainer, whatever. I was ready for that. I'd rehearsed that fight in my head a hundred times."

He paused.

"But it wasn't a man."

I looked at him in the mirror. He was staring at his hands.

"It was a woman," he said. "And the messages... man, they were detailed. Intimate. Talking about places they'd been, things they'd done. Plans for next time."

"You confront her?" I asked.

"Not yet. I don't even know how to confront her. Like, what do I even say? Hey babe, I know you're cheating with some bitch, how do I do that?"

He laughed, but there was no humor in it.

"I don't even know what that means," he said. "Like, is she gay? Was she always gay? Did I do something? Did I miss something?"

"Maybe it's not about you," I offered.

He looked at me sharp. "How's it not about me? I'm her husband."

"Exactly. You're her husband. Not her keeper. Not her mirror. Sometimes people discover parts of themselves that got buried a long time ago. Sometimes it's got nothing to do with you and everything to do with them finally telling themselves the truth."

He sat with that.

"Yeah, well," he said, voice tight. "Her truth is burning my whole life down."

The next rides were quiet. He'd pull up the hood on his jacket in summer like he was cold from the inside. I would see him type a message then erase it. Type again. Erase again. There is a kind of grief that has no words. You can smell it before you can name it.

A week later, Marcus called me directly. Not through the service. My personal line.

"I need a favor," he said.

"What kind of favor?"

"I need you to follow her."

"Follow her?" I said no, That's not what I do. I'm a driver, not a private investigator. But something in his voice made me pause.

"Marcus, "

"Please," he said. "I just need to know. I need to see it. Otherwise, it's just in my head. I'm going crazy, man. I need proof. I need to know I'm not making this up."

I thought about it. Thought about what my father used to say. Some people don't hire you to drive. They hire you to witness.

"Alright," I said. "But just once. After that, you handle it however you need to handle it."

"Once is all I need."

The following Thursday, I parked two blocks from his house, engine off, windows cracked. Suburbs were cooling down for the night, but it was still hot. Sprinklers clicked. A dog barked at nothing. Diane left at 6:47 PM. Hair done, makeup light, dressed like she was meeting a friend for drinks. Nothing too fancy, but intentional.

I followed her to a wine bar in Montrose. She parked, checked her phone, waited five minutes, then went inside.

I waited.

Ten minutes later, a woman showed up. Mid-thirties, natural hair, confident walk. Soft denim jacket, simple earrings, no ring. Not flashy, but present. The kind of woman any man would trip out over. I hoped this is just two friends having cocktails.

They hugged at the door. Damn, she met her at the door and didn't wait for her to find her I thought. Not long, but familiar. The kind of hug that says I've been waiting to see you. A since of longing.

I texted Marcus. She's here. Montrose. Wine bar off Westheimer.

He replied immediately. On my way.

Don't, bring your ass down here. You got me in this shit. I texted back. Let me handle this.

Three dots. Then: Fine. But I need details.

I went inside.

The place was dim, intimate, small tables with candles. Jazz playing low in the background. A chalkboard menu with wines I couldn't pronounce. Couples talking in whispers like the room trained them to. I took a seat at the bar, ordered a ginger ale, and watched their reflection in the mirror behind the bottles.

They weren't hiding. Weren't sneaking. They sat across from each other, leaning in, laughing, talking like old friends catching up. But every so often, their hands would touch. Light. Brief. Intentional. The kind of touch that says I know your story without you saying a word.

A server set down two glasses. Diane sniffed hers and smiled. The other woman told a story that made Diane cover her mouth to laugh. No guilt in that laugh. No flinch. Thirty minutes in, Diane reached across the table and held the woman's hand. Not secretive. Not quick. She just held it.

The other woman smiled.

Diane smiled back.

And in that moment, I saw something I wasn't expecting.

Peace.

Diane looked happy. Not guilty. Not conflicted. Just present. Like for the first time in a long time, she was exactly where she wanted to be.

The bartender asked if I wanted another. I shook my head, left cash on the bar, and walked out.

I called Marcus from the car.

"Well?" he said, voice tight.

"She's there. With her."

"And?"

"And they're just talking. Holding hands. Nothing explicit."

"That's enough," he said. "That's all I needed to know."

Silence.

"You alright?" I asked.

"No," he said. "But I will be."

He hung up.

Two days passed. Then three. He did not book. I figured he was wrestling the demon and the demon was wrestling back.

Two weeks later, Marcus called again. Asked if I could pick him up. Said he needed to talk and a ride to the airport.

When I pulled up, he looked different. Tired, but lighter. Like he'd been carrying something heavy and finally put it down.

"I confronted her," he said as soon as he got in.

"How'd it go?"

"Worse than I thought. And better."

He rubbed his face.

"She didn't deny it. Didn't make excuses. Just said she'd been trying to figure herself out for years and didn't know how to tell me."

"What'd you say?"

"I asked her if she ever loved me. She said yes. Said she still does. But not the way I need her to."

He looked out the window.

"She said she's been living a life that felt like it belonged to someone else. And she's tired of pretending."

"That's deep," I said.

"Yeah. But you know what the crazy part is?"

"What?"

"I believe her. And I don't even hate her for it."

He exhaled long and slow.

"I'm hurt. I'm angry. I feel like an idiot. But I don't hate her. Because I saw it, man. As we were talking. I saw her face. The way Diane spoke about Tiffany, that's her name. She looked free. And I realized I don't remember seeing her look like that with me."

He wiped his eyes.

"I don't know what happens next. We got kids. We got a house.

We got a whole life built. But I can't make her stay in a life that's killing her. Even if it kills me to let her go."

He told me about the kitchen table conversation. How they waited until the kids were at a friend's house. How Diane said the words slowly so they would be true. How Marcus folded his hands because he did not trust them to behave. How there were long pauses that were not empty, just full of old promises. They agreed to counseling for a season, then mediation. They would tell the kids together. They would not weaponize love.

They separated three months later. Quiet. Respectful. No public drama. They told the kids together, worked out custody, split everything fair. There were tears in the car after the recital. There were small holidays done twice. There were mornings when he woke up reaching for a ring that was not there and afternoons when he laughed and did not feel guilty about it.

Marcus moved into a loft downtown. Started therapy. Started working out. Started, slowly, figuring out who he was when he wasn't somebody's husband. He swapped the heavy watch for a simple one. He started cooking on Sundays. He learned the difference between alone and lonely. He started meeting his son for basketball in the park on Wednesdays and taught his daughter how to check the air in her bike tires. He made space where anger used to live.

There was a night he called me late from the bar. I picked him up and took him home, then he just sat in the backseat while I idled at the curb.

"You ever notice how quiet can be loud?" he asked.

"All the time."

"I hear the ice maker. The elevator. My neighbor's laugh. I keep waiting to hear her keys in the door and I know they are not coming. It's like my brain keeps checking an old lock."

"That fades," I said. "Or it changes shape."

"I hope so," he said. "I'm trying not to break under things that already broke."

We sat in silence for a while. He tipped big and walked in the building slow, like his bones were remembering how to carry him alone.

I picked him up for last time about a few years later.

He looked good. Healthy. Centered. Beard lined tight. New suit that fit like he meant it.

"How you been?" I asked.

"Better," he said. "Still hard. But better."

"You seeing anybody?"

He laughed. "Nah. Not ready. Still trying to figure out what I even want."

He paused.

"But I saw Diane last week. At our daughter's recital. She brought Tiffany."

"How was that?"

"Awkward at first. But then our daughter came over and hugged all three of us, and it was just life. You know?"

I nodded.

"She's happy," he said. "Really happy. And our kids are good. And that's all that matters."

He looked at me in the rearview.

"You were right, by the way. It wasn't about me. It was about her finding herself. And I had to let go of my ego long enough to see that."

We pulled up to his building. He did not get out right away. Just stared at the lobby lights.

"You ever think about the cost of freedom?" he asked.

"All the time."

"I thought freedom was about running toward something. Turns out sometimes it is about standing still and letting someone go without making them the villain."

He got out. Closed the door gentle. Walked in like a man who finally knew which floor was his.

I still think about Marcus sometimes. About how easy it is to mistake someone else's journey for a betrayal of your own. About how a driver becomes a witness, and a witness learns to keep both hands on the wheel when the story wants to swerve.

He didn't get the ending he wanted. But he got the truth. And sometimes that's harder. And more valuable.

Because love isn't about holding on.

It's about knowing when to let go. Here is what the road taught me. Secrets rot in dark places. Truth does not always heal right away, but it stops the rot. You cannot love someone into a shape that fits a story they were never meant to live. You can only love them as they are or let them go be it somewhere else. And if you are blessed, the kids will see three adults choose peace over pride and learn that home is not a single address. Home is how you treat each other when it gets hard.

Now, like I said at the start, this stays between us. Because some stories aren't lessons. They're just life. And life don't always wrap up neat. Sometimes it just unfolds, messy and real, and all you can do is watch, listen, and drive.

ELEVEN
THE WEDDING

Now check this out.

Before we get into this one, let me be clear: weddings are a whole different beast. You think you have seen people at their best and worst? Wait until you drive a wedding. That is when you find out who folks really are. Put an open bar, extra feelings, and a DJ with questionable taste in one room, and suddenly everybody thinks they are either in love or need to be.

I have done my share of weddings over the years. Driven brides who cried the whole way to the venue. Driven grooms who looked like they were heading to a parole hearing instead of an altar. I have seen bridesmaids fistfight in the back of a limo and groomsmen pass out before the ceremony even started.

But this wedding?

This one was different. Because this was not just another booking. This was the Hogans. And the Hogans were family.

Not by blood, but by years. By trust. By the kind of relationship you build one ride at a time until suddenly you are not just their driver anymore. You are the person they call when something matters or just to say hello.

I had been driving Mr. Hogan for close to eight years. Started with airport runs, then corporate events, then family occasions. Graduations. Anniversaries. The kind of people who remember your birthday and ask about your mother.

So when Todd and Emma Hogan's daughter Jasmine got engaged they called me about the wedding, there was no question. I was in. Not just as a vendor, but as someone who genuinely wanted to see this day go perfect.

"We want you handling everything," Mrs. Hogan said. "Transportation, coordination, all of it. If anyone can make this flawless, it is you."

No pressure, right?

Here is the thing. When people you care about trust you with something this big, you do not just show up. You show out. Because if I pulled off a seamless, stress free wedding day for two hundred guests, it was not only about one event. It was about building reputation. About proving I could handle the big jobs. About opening doors I had not even imagined yet.

So I went all in.

Four thirty passenger shuttle buses for guest transport. Two Mercedes Sprinter vans for the wedding party. And for the bride and groom, a white Rolls Royce Phantom that looked like it floated.

Everything planned to the minute. Routes mapped. Drivers briefed. Backups for the backups.

The venue was Houston Oaks Country Club & Retreat out in Hockley, an exquisite location over 1000 acres, oak trees that still look beautiful that are over 200 years old and a 15th century French Chapel, the kind of place that makes you feel like you stepped into a Southern fairy tale. Ceremony and reception both on-site, which simplified logistics. Hotel was about fifteen minutes away in Waller for the out-of-town guests.

I had it locked.

Or so I thought.

Because weddings do not follow plans.

Weddings follow chaos.

The day started smooth as silk.

I picked up Jasmine from her parents' house at 9 am. She looked like she'd walked out of a dream, and she wasn't even made up yet. Just in her jogging pants and a t-shirt with a robe. Dress was already at the facility along with her "glam squad" as she called them. She was glowing. I was too.

Mrs. Hogan was crying before we made it to the car.

"My baby," she kept saying, dabbing her eyes. "My beautiful baby."

Mr. Hogan stood with his hands in his pockets, trying to keep it together. He looked at me and gave a small nod that said take care of her. I nodded back. No words needed.

Jasmine climbed into the Rolls like she was born to ride in it.

"You ready for this?" I asked, catching her eye in the rearview.

She took a deep breath and smiled so wide I thought her face might split. "I have been ready my whole life."

"Then let us get you married."

The ceremony was perfect. Not a hitch. Jasmine floated down the aisle like she was walking on air. The groom, Devon Smith, looked at her like she was the only person in the world. Even I felt a lump in my throat, and I am not new to this.

Vows exchanged. Rings on. The preacher said, "You may kiss the bride," and Devon went for it like his life depended on it. The crowd erupted.

Beautiful.

The ceremony is the calm before the storm. Once the "I do" is done, people stop performing and start being themselves.

Cocktail hour set up on the terrace overlooking the grounds. Open bar, shrimp cocktail, those two bite appetizers that cost like a car note. String quartet in the corner. Everything elegant and calm.

The plan was simple: guests would enjoy cocktail hour for 90 minutes while the wedding party took photos around the property. Then they would transition everyone into the ballroom for dinner, toasts, and dancing. And I would ensure all guest would get to their perspective places at the end of the night.

Simple. Ah, not quite, but it sounds good.

Except nothing stays simple when you add alcohol and emotions.

Forty minutes into cocktail hour, the first ripple hit.

I was by the Rolls going over the evening timeline with my drivers when Tommy, one of my Sprinter guys, came jogging over with that face that says something is about to go left.

"We got a situation," he said low.

"What kind?"

"The bridesmaids."

Of course.

"What about them?"

"They are not at the photo shoot." I looked at him. "What do you mean they're not at the photo shoot? The photographer's got them on the schedule right now." Did you tell the wedding coordinator?

"Yeah, well, three of them vanished. And I can't find the coordinator either." I know you are saying this is not the job of the drivers, but like I said, this is family. I watched Jasmine grow up so I would take on any role that was needed of me. Hell, I'll walk her ass down the isle if Todd needed me to. I rubbed my temples. "Vanished where?"

"Vanished where?"

"If I knew, I would not say vanished."

I found them in the parking lot. Dresses hitched, heels in hand, trying to wave down an Uber.

"Ladies," I called, keeping my voice calm. "Where y'all think y'all are going?"

The tall one, Kendra, spun around with a guilty smile. "Oh, hey! We are just running out for food. We will be right back."

"Food."

"Those appetizers are cute, but they are not filling. We are starving."

"The reception dinner is in an hour and a half. Full plated meal. Steak, chicken, the works."

She looked at me like I had canceled Christmas. "An hour and a half? We cannot wait that long."

Another bridesmaid chimed in. "There is a Whataburger ten minutes away. Super quick."

"Y'all are in bridesmaid dresses."

"So?"

They were serious.

"Alright," I said. "Cancel the Uber. You are not riding to Whataburger in a random Camry. Tommy will take you in the Sprinter."

Kendra's eyes lit up. "Really?"

"Really. Because if y'all disappear and Jasmine finds out. Let's just say I'm not having it. And I'm not about to let three bridesmaids in fancy dresses ruin eight years go missing on my watch "You are the best," one squealed.

"Whatever" I laughed

Tommy blinked at me when I told him. "You want me to take bridesmaids to Whataburger. In the Sprinter."

"Yep."

"During cocktail hour."

"You want to argue or drive?"

He sighed. "Back in fifteen."

They made it in eighteen. Kendra had a ketchup dot on her dress and hid it under her bouquet. Crisis averted.

That was round one.

Round two hit during the shift from terrace to ballroom.

Guests moved smoothly. The wedding party lined up for the big entrance. My backup shuttle driver, Shawn, radioed in.

"Hey boss, we got a vibe situation."

"A what?"

"One groomsman plugged his phone into the bus speakers and declared himself the hype man. He is taking requests. It is all old school R and B. People are singing."

"Anybody complaining?"

"Nope."

"Let him cook. If the aunties start frowning, cut it."

"Copy."

Dinner went off clean. Toasts were heartfelt. Mr. Hogan's speech had half the room in tears and the other half pretending not to be. First dance was tender. Photographer was eating.

Then the DJ started the real party.

Within twenty minutes, the dance floor was packed. I'm talking shoulder-to-shoulder, multi-generational, no-inhibitions packed. Devon's grandmother was doing the mashed potato, don't ask me, but she was doing it. Somebody's uncle was doing the Cupid Shuffle like he'd been training for it but he kept going the wrong direction and bumping into everyone. Jasmine's little cousins were flossing in the corner taking selfies and on TikTok.

The wedding party, though, started disappearing.

An hour into dancing I came up four short. Two bridesmaids. Two groomsmen. Missing.

Bathroom. Terrace. Nowhere.

Then I heard music. Faint. From the parking lot.

One Sprinter. Door closed. Windows fogged. Bass thumping.

I knocked.

The music stopped.

Door cracked. Kendra peeped out. "Oh. Hey."

"You know there is a DJ inside," I said.

"Yeah, but he keeps playing the Cha Cha Slide. We are not doing number six."

"So you started a private party in my van."

A groomsman leaned into view, grinning. "Come on, we are not hurting anything."

I looked. Shoes off. Drinks in hand. Bluetooth speaker going. A small after party.

I thought about forcing them back in. Then the ballroom doors opened and the Cha Cha Slide hit again.

"Twenty minutes," I said. "Then cake. Deal?"

"Deal."

I closed the door and walked away, shaking my head.

Kids these days.

The real story showed up at ten.

I was doing what I do, looking around, that's when I realized someone else was missing.

Not a bridesmaid. Not a groomsman.

Uncle Dennis. The groom's uncle from the Smith side. Big personality. The one who had been telling the bartender to surprise him since six.

Tommy radioed. "Boss, second Sprinter. Might want to see this yourself."

The second Sprinter was supposed to be locked and empty. It was not.

Tommy stood outside like he had seen a ghost. "I heard voices. Thought it was kids. Opened it and..."

He waved a hand at the door.

I opened it.

Uncle Dennis on his knees with her legs on his shoulders. His shirt half unbuttoned. Panties on his head, sunglasses on, tilted slightly and his tie dangling down the middle of his chest. A woman I recognized from cocktail hour laying spread out wide, with her breast exposed to the stars.

They both froze.

"Evening," I said, voice flat.

Uncle Dennis turned and flashed a smile, face glistening. "Hey there, driver man."

"Sir," I said, "this is not the place for that. Your family is inside. People are going to come looking. Let us get you back before this turns into a situation."

As he got himself together, he lifted his fingers to his nose and said "Whew. That was fresh."

The woman tried not to laugh. Then realized I was not laughing and sat up straight. She's back fastened down, she did that surprisingly fast actually, I was impressed.

"Here is what we are going to do," I said. "You are going to step out first. You are going to walk straight back to the the restroom, wash your hand and face and gargle some water or whiskey at least. In five minutes, ma'am, you will follow. Separate paths. No detours. We are going to pretend I checked a taillight. Nobody seen you except us so nobody will know. Cool?

Uncle Dennis nodded. "You are all business. I like that."

"Great. Feet on the ground, sir."

He stood, straightened his tie, and checked his reflection in the window like he had been outside for air. He headed in without turning around.

Five minutes later, she followed. Clean face. Neutral expression. Mission accomplished.

Tommy let out a breath. "Weddings are wild."

"You have no idea."

Cake cutting. Bouquet toss. Garter toss. Last dance under the stars on the terrace.

At midnight, Jasmine and Devon made their exit. Sparklers lined the walkway. Guests cheered. I rolled them to the hotel in at the IAH in the Rolls, windows cracked, night air cool, two newlyweds laughing in the back like they were the only people in the world. Their flight was set for 8am.

At the hotel, Jasmine leaned forward. "Thank you," she said. "You helped made today perfect."

"That is what I am here for."

"No, really," she said. "My parents told me how much you handled. I am glad you were part of this."

Devon shook my hand. "Appreciate you, man."

I watched them head inside, arms around each other, still in their wedding clothes, and felt something I do not always feel after a job.

Pride. Not only because it went smooth. Because I had been trusted with something that mattered. And I delivered.

Back at Houston Oaks I rounded up the Sprinters. Kendra and two bridesmaids were asleep in the first van. Shoes off. Makeup smudged. One of them holding a piece of cake like a trophy. I did not wake them. I got them safely to the hotel.

Uncle Dennis was back on the dance floor by the end. He stuck to water after a few whiskey gargles. Smart man.

Two weeks later Mrs. Hogan called.

"I wanted to thank you again," she said. "People are still talking about how smooth it all ran."

"Happy to do it."

"My sister is planning her daughter's wedding next year. Three hundred guests. She needs someone who can run logistics. Interested?"

"Yes, ma'am."

See, that is the thing about doing something right. It is not about the one job. It is about the doors it opens. The trust it builds. The reputation that carries you into the next room. Jasmine's wedding could have been a mess. Bridesmaids on a burger run. A rogue dance party in a van. Uncle Dennis running a tongue Olympics in the van. None of it touched the bride and groom. None of it ruined the day.

Because that is the job.

You handle the chaos so they can have the fairy tale.

Not because you are the cheapest.

Not because you are the flashiest.

But because you are the one people trust when it matters most.

Weddings, man.

Everybody thinks it is about the ceremony, the dress, the cake.

The real story lives in the margins.

In the Sprinter vans. In the parking lots. In the moments nobody is supposed to see.

And me? I see it all. Somebody has to keep the chaos from spilling into the fairy tale. That somebody is me. Now, like I said at the start, this stays between us. Because some stories are not lessons. They are just life. Messy. Funny. Human. And if you are lucky, you get to witness it.

TWELVE
THE PROM

My phone is blowing up. Just sitting here. Scared. Afraid. Not knowing what to do next. Emotions on overdrive. Why did I say yes is what I thought. I'm sitting at my office desk, affectionately known as my dining room table, staring at the screen, heart pounding, knowing that every buzz means something went wrong.

The number keeps flashing. Winnie, Texas.

I answer the first call.

"Hello?"

"The kids are going to miss the prom!" The voice is tight, controlled, but I can hear the pain underneath. How did this happen? The line goes dead before I can respond.

My stomach drops.

Let me back up.

The call came two weeks earlier from a man in Winnie, Texas, about an hour east of Houston if the traffic's good, longer if the rain gets in the way. His voice carried both pride and worry, the kind that lives in folks who have worked hard their whole lives but still want to give their children more than they had. He explained that three families were pitching in for a single stretch limousine. Not an SUV, not a sedan, a real stretch.

Now, most people don't realize the old-school limos are basically dinosaurs. They look nice in pictures, but they're a headache to maintain and drive. I didn't own one, so I had to subcontract through another company. I told him I'd handle everything and that the kids would be in great hands. Before ending the call and giving the deposit, he laid down the one non-negotiable rule.

"Make sure the driver takes the ferry."

I repeated it back to him. "The ferry. Got it."

"You got it," he said.

The plan was simple: dinner first, pictures second, then the prom, then home. He even sent me a photo of the kids, tuxes sharp, dresses bright, and a black stretch limousine clean and elegant. You could tell these families had sacrificed to make this happen. That meant the world to me.

Growing up, I didn't go to my own prom. My mother couldn't afford it. I wasn't going to press her or bring it up because I knew we didn't have it like that. I played like I was too cool for prom and I would just skip it. "You lames can have that," I remember saying. So when I saw that photo, I saw myself. I saw what it meant for parents to scrape together enough to give their kids one perfect night. I wasn't about to let them down.

Now here I am, six months out from leaving The Airline, sitting at my desk with my phone lighting up like a crisis hotline, and I know. I already know. I let them down.

I call the driver.

No answer.

I call again. And again.

On the fourth try, he picks up.

"Yeah?"

"Where the hell are you?" I say, trying to keep my voice steady.

"We hit some flooding," he says, like he's reporting the weather. "Road's blocked. We're just sitting here waiting for it to clear."

"What road?"

He names some back route I've never heard of.

"Why aren't you on the ferry?" I say.

Silence.

"I told you to take the ferry. Why the hell are you on a back road? Who takes a back road in a place they've never been to?"

"Ferry had a wait," he says. "I thought I could save time."

I close my eyes. Take a breath. Try not to lose it.

"How long have they been sitting there?"

"About an hour."

"An hour? And you're just now telling me?"

"I thought it would clear."

"Is it clearing?"

"Not yet."

I want to reach through the phone and choke this bastard. But that wouldn't get those kids to the prom. That wouldn't fix anything.

"How long till the water drops?"

"I don't know. Another hour, maybe two."

"They're gonna miss the whole thing."

"I know. I'm sorry."

Sorry. Like that was supposed to mean something.

I hang up and sit there in the quiet, my heart pounding so hard I could feel it in my throat.

I didn't know what to do.

I thought about calling the father back, but what was I supposed to say? "Yeah, your kids are stuck in a flood because the driver I hired didn't follow instructions"? I thought about getting in my car and driving out there myself, but by the time I got to Winnie, the prom would be over. And what was I gonna do when I got there anyway? "Hey kids, swim this way!" Y'all know my Black ass can't swim. I thought about refunding the money, but that wouldn't give those kids their night back.

So I just sat there.

Staring at my phone.

Watching the minutes tick by.

Hating myself.

But I called the dad anyway.

He answered on the first ring.

"What's going on?"

"The driver took a back road," I said. "They're stuck. The road flooded. I'm so sorry. I told him to take the ferry and he, "

"How long?"

"At least another hour. Maybe two. They're going to miss the prom."

Silence on the other end. The kind that's heavier than yelling.

"I'll refund everything," I said quickly. "The whole amount. I don't care what it costs me. This is on me and I, "

"Just get them home safe," he said, and hung up.

I sat up the rest of the night, wide awake, running numbers in my head. The limo rental. The deposit. The families' money. If they sued, I'd lose everything. If they blasted me online, I'd never book another job. Six months in, and I was about to be done.

I kept thinking about my mother. About how she would go and clean other people's houses just so the starvation ghost wasn't sitting in our kitchen. About how hard she tried.

These people probably spent their last to make sure their kids had their night. This wasn't some kids from Royal Oaks who could literally afford a helicopter to get their kids to the prom on time. And now I'd done let down these families. Those poor kids.

Around midnight, the driver called again.

"Water's dropping. We're moving."

"Where are you taking them?"

"Back to Winnie. Prom's over."

I didn't say anything. Just hung up.

The driver texted at 1:30 a.m. and said that the kids were at home and safe. These kids sat there for five hours.

First thing in the morning, the father called. "Oh shit," I said, because I wanted to beat him and call him first.

I let it ring twice before I answered.

"Hello?" His voice was quiet. Tired.

"You already know the kids didn't make the prom," he said. "But I tell you, they had one hell of a night."

I blinked. "What?"

"Yeah, it was a rocky start. The driver cranked up the tunes, had some chips and sodas in the trunk. They got out of the car, stood in the rain, danced right there on the side of the road in their dresses and tuxes. Took pictures. Sang. And the driver even tried to rap and show his dance moves. My daughter said it was the best part of the whole night."

I didn't know what to say.

"Your guy made the best of the situation, and it worked," he continued. "And they're home. They're safe. That's what matters."

"But, "

"The driver made a mistake," he said. "But you didn't. You set it up right. You told him what to do. He just didn't listen. That's on him, not you."

I felt something crack open in my chest.

"I still want to refund you," I said.

"How about we split it," he said. "Fifty-fifty. That's fair."

"You don't have to, "

"I know I don't have to. But that's what's right. Your guy's night was almost done. He had already taken them to eat and to take pictures, and from that end, I can see why he went that way. The ferry would have taken longer. I'm not looking for a free ride, and if it didn't end up raining, it would have been a great decision. So half is fair."

I agreed.

I refunded 50% of the fare and thanked him for his honesty and insight.

After we hung up, I sat at that desk. Stared at the wall. Just sitting.

I thought about grace. About how this man could've buried me. Could've taken everything. And instead, he met me halfway. I thought about those kids dancing in the rain. This idiot out in the rain with the kids, trying to make their night the best that it could be. Damn MC Raindrop. About how they turned a disaster into a memory. About how resilience doesn't always look like success; sometimes it just looks like making the best of what you got.

I thought about my mother. About all the times she couldn't give me what I wanted, but she gave me what I needed. And somehow, that was enough.

Prom night taught me that silence isn't just about keeping secrets. Sometimes it's about shutting up long enough to let grace speak first.

And sometimes, the best stories aren't the ones where everything goes right. They're the ones where everything goes wrong, and people somehow get it right.

THIRTEEN
NEW YEAR EVE

You remember back in 2019 when I made that post about me driving Cedric The Entertainer on New Year Eve? He was performing at the Smart Financial Center out in Sugar Land off 59 with Nephew Tommy, Arnez J, and D.L. Hughley.

Now don't get it twisted. I haven't had that many drinks that I'm about to start naming names and get my Black ass sued. Naw, this story ain't about Cedric. He was cool. Professional. Tipped well. Did his job, I did mine. This story is about what I didn't show.

The night started how most celebrity gigs start, smooth and boring. Trying to get everything right because every impression is a lasting one. Picked Cedric up from the hotel around seven. Black Escalade, windows tinted dark enough to keep nosy folks out his business. He climbed in the back, phone already out, answering texts and emails like a man who don't get a day off even on New Year's Eve.

"How you doing tonight?" I asked.

"I'm good, brother. Just ready to put in this work."

That was it. No small talk. No stories. Just a man getting ready to do what he do. I respected that.

We rolled down 59 toward Sugar Land. Traffic wasn't bad yet; most folks were still at home getting dressed or pre-gaming before they hit the clubs. The Smart Financial Center sat out there like a spaceship, all glass and lights. By the time we pulled up, the parking lot was half full and security was posted up thick.

I took him through the special entrance. VIP access. No crowds, no cameras, just a regular door and a hallway that smelled like new carpet and Cheetos. Other drivers were pulling in, black Escalades, Sprinters, a couple of those fancy Mercedes sedans that cost more than my whole business. Celebrities and their teams moving like ants at a picnic, everybody on a mission.

I walked in with Cedric and his team, then posted up in the hallway outside of the greenroom area where all the drivers and staff hung out. That's when I saw him.

Big Sip.

Now let me tell you about Big Sip.

He was the biggest, blackest, and ugliest motherfucker you ever saw in your life. I'm talking six feet tall, easy five hundred pounds, skin so dark it looked like he absorbed light. Face like a bulldog that got stung by bees. Gut hanging over his belt like he was smuggling a whole Thanksgiving dinner under his shirt.

Ok, I'm being mean... But if I said he had double-D-size breasts would that be ok?

Ok, ok, ok, I'll stop, but one thing I will say, that motherfucker was funny as hell.

I mean the kind of funny where you laughing so hard you forget to breathe. The kind of funny where your stomach hurt and your face hurt and you don't even care because whatever he just said was worth it.

He was the kind of person that if you had a weak bladder you would have to leave because your ass would surely piss your pants and be ashamed.

He wasn't part of the show. Wasn't on the lineup. Wasn't anybody's plus-one as far as I could tell. He was just there, posted up in the back with a plate of wings, chilling like he owned the place.

And nobody knew who he came with.

I asked one of the other drivers, "Who's that?"

Dude shrugged. "Hell if I know. Thought he was with you."

Nobody knew who this motherfucker was.

During the show, I'm sitting in a room off the hallway scrolling through my phone when Big Sip plops down next to me. You should've heard that couch scream for dear life.

"Big Homie, you a driver?" he asked, voice deep like he gargled gravel.

Now I'm thinking, did THIS motherfucker just call ME BIG? Ain't no way.

"Yeah," I said.

"Who you driving?"

"Can't say."

He grinned. "I respect that. You a Bro-fessional. Top-secret squirrel-ass nigga. Yo ass ain't driving OBAMA, you can tell me who you driving."

"Nah Big Worm, I mean Squirm, Chips, what yo name is again?"

"Ha! Yo ugly ass got jokes, I like you, Big Homie."

He leaned back, wings in one hand, napkin in the other. "You ever think about how wild it is that we just accept New Year's Eve as a thing?"

I looked at him. "What?"

"Like, we all just agreed that December thirty-first at midnight, we gonna act brand new. Fresh start. New year, new me. But it's just a date, bro. Ain't nothing magic about this shit. We could pick any day. Could be May nineteenth. Could be October second. But nah, we all decided on some bullshit like December thirty-first is when we pretend we gonna change."

I laughed. "Sip, what are you talking about?"

"I'm saying!" He waved the chicken wing like a professor with a pointer. "And then we make resolutions we know we ain't keeping. 'I'm gonna lose weight.' 'I'm gonna save money.' 'I'm gonna call my mama more.' Two weeks in, we back to eating Popeyes and ignoring her calls."

"You got a resolution, Big Sip?" I asked.

"Nah, Big Homie. I don't do no damn resolutions. I ain't letting these bitches go, I ain't eating no rabbit food, talking 'bout I'ma lose some weight. I'm doing the opposite. I'm getting two bad bitches and going to Steak 'n Shake."

"Where the hell you gonna find a Steak 'n Shake?"

"Hell if I know, but wherever I go it's gonna be with two bad bitches."

"I ain't finished my shit, don't even get me started on the countdown," he continued. "Ten, nine, eight, why we counting down? If it's a celebration, shouldn't we count up? Like, 'One! Two! Three! Happy New Year, MOTHER FUCKERS!' Make it feel like we building to something instead of running out of time."

I was crying. "Sip, you trippin'."

"I'm just calling it how I see this shit."

Big Sip stayed backstage. He didn't watch from the wings. Didn't sneak out to the seats. Just stayed in the greenroom eating and talking to whoever wandered by. And everybody who talked to him walked away laughing.

I went to get something to drink from the SUV. As I was walking back in, some dude was about to sit on Sip.

"What you doing, motherfucker? Oh hell naw, you gotta get yo ass out of here!"

The dude burst out laughing. "I thought yo big ass was the couch. Open your fucking eyes so we can see your Black ass."

The room erupted with laughter. Sip couldn't do anything but laugh too. It was a good one. But he did take up most of the couch.

Moments before midnight hit, we all gathered in the hallway to count down to the New Year. I look at Big Sip and his ass is the ONLY one yelling, "1, 2, 3... I'm building shit, niggas!"

People laugh, people are drinking, just a natural good time.

About 20 minutes later, I walked Cedric out, loaded him up, and we headed back to the hotel. Clean. Easy. Professional.

But the whole ride, I kept thinking about Big Sip.

Who was he? How'd he get back there? And why the hell was he so damn funny?

A couple days later, I'm telling the story to a buddy of mine who works security at different venues around Houston.

"Big Sip?" he said. "You talking about the big Black dude who just shows up places?"

"Yeah."

"Man, that dude's a legend. He been doing that shit for years. Nobody knows how he gets in, but he always does. Never causes trouble. Just eats, talks shit, makes people laugh, then disappears."

"So nobody knows who he is?"

"Nope. And honestly, I don't think anybody cares. He's like a good-luck charm or something. If Big Sip's backstage, you know the show's gonna be good."

I sat with that for a minute.

"Y'all ever try to stop him?"

My buddy laughed. "You seen that motherfucker? Who stopping him, and why would we? He ain't hurting nobody. And half the time, the talent don't even know he's there. He just vibes."

I never saw Big Sip again after that night. But every New Year's Eve since, I think about him. About how some people just exist in spaces they're not supposed to be in, and somehow, it all works out. About how sometimes the best part of a night ain't the headliner or the countdown or the champagne.

Sometimes it's just a five-hundred-pound dude with a plate of wings and a theory about why we count down instead of up.

Happy New Year, Sip. I'm building shit!

FOURTEEN
THE LEGACY

S hiiid, I been sitting here with you running my mouth, telling you everybody else's business and realized I haven't shared my story with you. Nah, let me stop lying, it's easy to tell other people's secrets but you don't want to tell your own. I've actually been dreading this chapter and thought about not talking to you about it, but what the hell, we all grown and your shit don't smell any better than mine.

I really don't know where to start, so I guess I'll start at the beginning.

Back in chapter one, I told you that it was my first fare; well that wasn't 100% true. Back in the late 90's I used to work with my dad driving Lincoln Town Cars. He would give me trips and I would take people where they needed to go. Same setup, the only difference was I was leasing a Town Car from someone that he knew, and I would pay them five hundred dollars a week for their car. Yeah, I know, I was getting robbed, but my father had a lot of business and I made easily three to four times that amount per week, so I was fine with it. Plus, I was planning on buying my own car as soon as I saved up enough money.

Like I mentioned in chapter 9, I ended up moving back to Chicago to make sure my brother was able to go to college and I could take care of my mother. I didn't want him to have any excuses for not taking the opportunity to go to college and she needed me there, although she would never admit it. Plus, she didn't have to admit it, it was my responsibility to take care of her. I would move heaven and earth to make sure she was straight at all times. I just pray that I did enough.

After her passing, an HR position opened up, and I was able to transfer to the Houston office. This was a huge transition for me; I was the only Black man in our office, if I'm not mistaken, for some time the only one on our floor. Some of my white relatives, because we're all family members now, might be thinking to themselves, why does that even matter? Underrepresentation matters. Imagine walking into a corporate office and you were the only white person there, most will be looking for a new job during their first break. Fortunately, I didn't have to. I had some of the greatest coworkers a person could ask for. Each one loved me in their own special way and it showed, and the ones that didn't, they still showed me respect and I believe they came around eventually. They were all special to me, and it is them that I miss the most, even more than the opportunity to fly around the world for free. Let me check my temperature, did I say that shit out loud?

Ok, I already told you about the 2.8 percent raise, so I won't rehash that bullshit.

What made me choose driving limousines? Well, I prayed about leaving the airline day in and out. There were three things, or people, I should say, that led me into starting a limo business. One being my pastor, Keion Henderson of the Lighthouse Church in Houston, TX. He always preached about entrepreneurship, owning your own, and one particular Sunday it was like the sanctuary went dark and he was speaking directly to me, pouring into my empty cup. I left full and overflowing with ideas, but I didn't know what I wanted or could do for that matter.

Then I met Willa Mae. Yes, she was an older woman, don't judge me. She was cute on her dating profile and I guess we connected at the right time. We met at a local Starbucks, and we had one of the best conversations. She was a well-respected doctor, with past TV shows and Emmys, and was just on top of her shit. I wasn't, so I soaked up everything she spilled.

I'm not gonna lie, I almost did it... but I looked down at her legs and saw those damn brown compression stockings, sock thingies, and there was no way I could get past that. Anyway, I'm getting off track. What she said to me stayed in my head constantly for a week. She looked at me and said, "What do you do again?" I told her that I was in HR and worked for the major airline. Her face turned upside down and scrunched up. "You don't look like you're in HR." Huh? I said inside my head. What the hell is she going with this, I thought. I would have thought promotions or something with the public. "I can't put my finger on it," she continued to say. "I'm hearing something, and you want to change things up." Now, when people start saying they are hearing from the Lord on my behalf, I usually tune them out. If I had a few dollars for every woman that said God told them that I was their husband, I'd be paid. People seem to love to lie on God. But there was something different about this conversation. She then stopped, took a sip of her coffee, and asked me, "If you could start a business right now what would it be?" Hell, I've been trying to figure that shit out for weeks now. "I don't know," I said. She laughed, then followed up by saying, "What do you know about right now, without a shadow of a doubt, you could do without even thinking about it?" And it clicked immediately. I can drive. I'm a damn good driver, and I know the limo business.

She said, "That's it. You have a servant's heart, that's what you should be doing."

The third one wasn't so spiritual, not in the sense of a word from God, but as I was doing Uber with my Chrysler 300, I was dressed in my suit and the passenger, out of nowhere, said, "Have you ever thought about starting your own car service? If you do, here's my card. I'll be your first client." And he was.

So what's next? More of the grind, of course. I did the Uber thing, learned the city a bit more, and was able to save up some money for a down payment on a new SUV.

Before I gave my resignation from the airline, I went to every doctor I could, because if I was going to quit my "high profile HR job," as people thought, I didn't want to quit, then find out I'm dying, got cancer, or some other crazy shit and not have insurance. After receiving a clean bill of health, I prepared for my exit. I didn't even have a suitable vehicle or name for the company.

I went to get an SUV. It was beautiful, just looking at me saying, pick me, you know you want me. The seduction was real, she wanted me and I wanted her, a black-on-black Cadillac Escalade ESV, that extended one with the extra booty, all the bells and whistles. She was sexy. But I was turned away due to bad credit, and they demanded a co-signer. There was no one I could ask, hell, ain't nobody gonna help me.

I knew that my brother's credit was better than mine, so I asked the guy if it could be anybody or it had to be an outstanding credit source. He laughed and said, with your down payment, it could pretty much be anybody. So I went to some dude outside and asked him... nah, I'm just playing. I went home and told my brother the situation. He said, let's do it. No questions asked, just, what do I have to do and where do I sign? And we got the SUV.

This is actually happening, I thought. I went home and thought about a name for the company. Since Proverbs 13:22 is my mantra, "A good man leaves behind an inheritance for his children's children," and I believe myself to be a good man, heck, I pray for it daily. So yes, I want to leave a legacy for my children's children. Legacy Executive Transportation Services LLC was born.

Giving my resignation wasn't as hard as I thought it would be. See, after she slid that 2.8% across the desk with pride, she then began to ask me my goals for the next year. You know how this shit goes, well, we see what the last review got me, but this was the first time that I have ever said, I don't have any goals for next year. I actually did, all ready to go through them with her as we did each year. "I don't have any goals for next year," I restated as I looked at her directly in her eyes without blinking. "You always are prepared with your goals and a plan for the upcoming year, that's how you always kill it," she said. I politely and genuinely said, I will not be here next year. After this review, I know this is not where I belong. I don't know when or where it will be, but I give you my word that it will not be a surprise. I will leave you prepared and will train anyone you need me to with full notice.

And that's what I did. I worked there about another month, and my last day was Friday, November 17, 2017. I only had one request of her. I did not want to be ineligible to return to work. I didn't want to burn any bridges. I spent 10 years there, and although I wouldn't be able to get my time back if I ever had to return, when I finally told people that I was leaving, some people started to act different towards me.

Some cold shoulders.

Some people saying I was crazy to leave the airline and go drive Uber because he damn sure ain't getting no limousine.

People are crazy, but you gotta love them. Not everybody can see your vision. I guess it's because it is not for them to see. Everyone can't be a leader, some have to manage and others just have to work, and depending on the season of life dictates where you are in that rotation.

I was born to do this.

Excerpt from Interview with Voyage Houston Magazine titled:

eet Orlandus Shorter of Legacy Executive Transportation Services in West Houston.

"It's funny how life happens. I had no clue that I would be in this business and even ran away from doing it full-time for years. My grandfather started as a yellow-cab driver over 50 years ago. Following in his footsteps, my dad also started as a yellow-cab driver, then transitioned into owning a town-car service for nearly 30 years, which I would drive for him from time to time. Now, here I am taking over the torch and pressing forward as Legacy Executive Transportation Service, LLC. My family has serviced the Houston area for over 50 years, wow, just saying that, it blows my mind.

Growing up on the West Side of Chicago, in my world, dreams were just dreamed, some of which were barely remembered and none placed into action. I've always wanted to be my own boss, not even knowing what that really meant. People use the term boss or entrepreneur so loosely that I never even thought of it as a real, obtainable goal. After the passing of my mother in 2011, I knew that it was time for me to leave Chicago and step outside of my comfort zone. Since I was working at the airline, I had the opportunity to receive a promotion and move to Houston in February 2012.

Over the next five years, in 2017, while at my desk, I looked around to find that I was at the same desk, same pay, and doing the same process for someone else's dream. That scared me. The following Sunday, my pastor was speaking about entrepreneurship, as he has done many times before, but this time I heard it differently. The next week, while having coffee, I was speaking to a lady at the Starbucks I was in, and as we talked and shared our stories, she stopped me and said, 'Have you ever thought about going into business for yourself? God is telling me that you should be doing something different.' Yes, I was blown away and a bit confused, but in speaking more with her, I realized that there was something that I could start right now, that I knew all about and had been doing for many years already, the limo business, which I founded in October 2017."

That was part of the interview, and yes, it's still online. And it is still funny how life happens. Now, almost ten years after starting a new chapter, another 14 or so started. I'm not into astrology, but I am kind of big on numbers, not on what they mean but what they say to me. I knew chapter 14 had to be this chapter, the chapter about me, about the legacy, and about my life, since I was born on June fourteenth. Little things like that I look for. Is that strange? Do you do that too? If you don't, don't start; I'm sure whatever you are doing is working for you if you were able to get this book.

So yeah, back to it. I didn't know my grandfather. I just knew his name , let's call him Lee Thompson. Although I didn't know him, I heard that Lee Thompson was a sharp dresser, loved brims (as do I), and he was an even harder worker. That's all that I actually know of him besides what you read in the excerpt.

As for my dad, I do know a little bit more. I had to laugh at myself on that one. As before, we will call him Otis Thompson, or you can call him Paw Paw. I think he would probably like that.

Otis is a tall, dark, and handsome mid-to-slender man. He's slow to speak and doesn't say much when he does speak, unless it's about God or sports, otherwise you may get ten or twenty words out of him. As you know, I worked with him from time to time. Sometimes business was good and other times it wasn't, but there are ebbs and flows in every business. When I started Legacy, Otis had easily been in business over 30 years and had driven some of Houston's elite. I've met the most wealthy people in my life through my dad, I mean unthinkable amounts of wealth, and most of them were not assholes. There were a few, but I won't put them in this set of stories.

With 30 years of experience, you would think that he would own the limousine industry in Houston. His counterparts do. I remember one time, I was trying to introduce a new idea to him for the business back when I was working for him, I shouldn't say working for; to be totally honest it was more like contracted with him, and he kept me fed. But when I gave my suggestion on how to do whatever it was regarding technology, he told me, "This is my business," and until it becomes your business, don't tell him what to do with his business. That was a major slap in the face to me. I truly wasn't trying to take over his business, I was just trying to help, truly help. I knew he should have been way further along in his business, but this wasn't a business, it was a job disguised as a business.

Unfortunately, that's many people. It happens all the time, mostly without people realizing it. So you can see why I did not work under his umbrella. We simply had different views when it came to business and technology. I really wished we could have combined forces and made something special.

NOW HEAR ME OUT, and please don't think I am throwing my dad under the bus. I love him without pause. He got me here. Although we don't have the best relationship, I honor and respect him. I am just telling you my story. His story may differ, he may call me an asshole of a son who tried to steal his empire, I don't know. I do know that there are multiple sides to every story, and this is my truth and I'm sharing it with you.

That wasn't the only occasion something like that would happen or be said, but not all the time. I guess I need more context here. I didn't grow up with my father. I didn't know him until I was 8 or 9, somewhere around there. I knew his cousin, that was more like a brother to him. He also lived in Chicago, so he would come get me and I would hang out with my dad's side of the family.

I remember growing up and people would say, Who is that?

"Oh, that's Otis' son!"

"Otis got a son?" they would respond.

Imagine hearing that over and over for years.

I never saw my mother and father in the same room until my mother was in her casket and he came to the funeral.

Again, this ain't that kind of story. The one thing I can say about him that I am grateful about is that he introduced me to Christ, and Jesus has been my Savior ever since. I can hear you now... not with all the cuss words you used... read your Bible... hold up a mirror... nobody is perfect... and some shit just feels better when it's accompanied with a few choice words.

So,

In my business, I got a lot of my business from my father in the beginning. I got some guidance from him, but a lot of stuff I had to learn on my own. Maybe because he forgot, didn't know, or a rule had changed. Either way, I had to hustle if I was going to continue to make it. I could not rely on my dad's business; I had to get it myself. As they say, I had to get that shit out the mud.

I would go to networking events, conferences, drive Uber in richer neighborhoods, talk to any and everybody. Some of you may remember, I used to blow your social media up about Legacy. I know y'all were tired of me, but I did not care. I wanted to be known. I was hungry. I was going to get it through hell or high water.

I didn't have much growing up, and moving to Houston I was finally making something of myself. I remember in Chicago we would be handing out turkeys at church, and I was the one that needed a damn turkey because we just didn't have it that year, month, day, or whatever. Oh, I remember going to the food pantry to get some food, and I would go faithfully until I saw Sister Howard from church working at the food pantry, MY food pantry! I saw her and I turned around before I could let her see the good ole Deacon that needed a handout. Damn you, Sister Howard! That was my food pantry, damnit!

Pride, I'll tell ya!

But we made the best of what we had. We didn't have much, but we had each other, and $647 a month from my mother's Social Security wasn't going to do nothing for her. So I hustled, worked, and did whatever I could do that wouldn't get my black ass killed or thrown in jail.

We made it happen. I also remember her trying to get on Section 8. Oh, for years she was on the list, climbing that damn list, wishing for the dream. She was the one that needed it, while I knew people that didn't, paying $1 rent. Damn you, one-dollar renters... LOL.

When she passed away, a week later the yellow envelope came with her packet for her Section 8. Her number was finally pulled. I guess they didn't realize that she had already found her home.

The Pivot

With all of the hard work, shit was starting to look up. I had my own client list: I was indexed in Google above the fold, that's where you are on the first page when people are looking for a limo company in Houston. I was getting calls in and not having to call out. Even my dad saw the shift. He asked me if I would mind if he got a license plate that said Legacy. My license plate said Legacy00. I didn't mind, because even without him saying anything, he was telling me that he sees it. He sees the vision. I was giving him work. Some people would leave him and come to me. My shit was different, custom bottled water, luxury sedans, I had a network of other luxury vehicles, and things were looking up. I was amazed at how things were looking, not just looking, I had a business and not just a job. I had contractors working for me, a network across the U.S., and a mentor that knew his shit and worked with me. I am forever grateful and humbled. So yes, he could get Legacy plates. It was an honor. He got his plates and it said OLEGACY.

Perfect choice. Was it his legacy, was it my legacy, it didn't matter; we share the same legacy, no matter how you look at it.

As I write this now, Legacy Executive Transportation Services, LLC is no longer in business. I don't know the name of his business, he changed the name often, but just kept the same number. Everyone knows Otis, so it works for him.

When COVID came along and the world shut down, that was it for me. I had just interviewed a driver for a new position I was hiring for after I had just picked up my box tickets for the Lizzo concert for the Rodeo. It was for Black Friday, as I like to call it. That's when the Rodeo would have a concert on a Friday with a Black artist, and Lizzo was the choice for that year. I wasn't a fan, but I took a strong liking to the Rodeo and who is going to pass up six free box tickets to the Rodeo? I was all in. Just as I was ending the interview, I received an alert on my phone that the Rodeo was shutting down due to COVID. I said, if they are shutting down the Houston Rodeo, shit is real, Dad, and I would not be hiring anyone. I thanked the interviewee and told him that I would reach out to him after the interview process was complete. I never interviewed anyone else. Shit was shutting down quick, and I knew that it would never be the same. I dealt with all corporate clients, no proms or specialty work. With all of the Zoom calls happening, I knew the cost savings would change the landscape of corporate travel forever. So sorry, interview dude, if you are reading this, shit got bad, and I pray that you made it.

But there was a saving grace in the whole COVID pandemic, the Hogans! They kept me going. The world was shut down and I wasn't getting any income coming in. I had to sell the truck that I had for the new driver and use that as survival money for my brother and me, just enough to keep us afloat for God only knows how long this shit would last. But the Hogans, those damn Hogans, they helped me so much over the years, and they didn't stop. I received a call from Mr. Hogan. He wanted to see how me and my brother were holding up through all of this. I told him my status and that things were not looking good. He got me and my brother tested for COVID and said that as long as we did not entertain guests, etc., that I could still drive him and his family until everything was lifted. I drove his wife to work and back to the ranch Monday through Friday for four hours a day and made more than enough to carry the load.

Can't nobody tell me there isn't a God. I am forever grateful to the Hogans.

I don't talk to them much now. Knowing the shift, after dropping the wife off at the office, I was sitting in an empty movie-parking-lot thinking of my next move. What could I possibly do where I don't have to spend years in school and have to start back over? Do I go back to the airline? What is my next move, Lord? Then I sat in silence. **Vrooom, vrooom, vrooom**, the sounds of 18-wheelers as they passed by on the interstate. I went to truck-driving school and received my CDL and became a truck driver. So I guess you can now call me The Silent Trucker. It's been five years now, and damn do I have more stories to tell.

My mother never got to see her oldest son start his own business, begin to hire people, or hear the stories firsthand. But I believe that she's seen it all and said, That damn son of mine is a natural-born fool. She might be right. I damn sure know she would be smiling with her head held high.

Hey Momma, I'M STILL BUILDING SHIT!

FIFTEEN

SHUT UP AND DRIVE

Check this out. Now this call came on a Tuesday afternoon while I was sitting in my truck outside a Starbucks in Montrose, waiting on a client who was running fifteen minutes late or so and texting apologies every three. I was scrolling through emails I didn't want to answer, half-listening to some podcast about conspiracy theories I didn't believe in, when my phone lit up with a number I didn't recognize. Chicago area code. 312. I stared at it for a second, thumb hovering over the decline button, then let it ring through to voicemail. Whoever it was could leave a message. If it mattered, they'd call back.

They did. Two minutes later, same number, same ring. This time I answered.

"Hello?"

Silence for a beat. Then a breath. Then a voice I hadn't heard in three years but recognized immediately, the way you recognize a song you used to know all the words to even if you haven't heard it since high school.

"Hey," she said.

Just that. Hey. Like we'd talked yesterday. Like three years was nothing. Like she hadn't disappeared from my life the day I packed up and transferred to the Houston office at The Airline and walked out of that building for the last time. My chest tightened before my brain even caught up. I sat up straighter in my seat, turned that bullshit off the radio, and stared out the windshield at nothing.

"It's me," Carla said, and I could hear the slight nervousness in her voice, like she wasn't sure I'd remember.

Like there was any chance I wouldn't.

"Yeah," I said. "I know."

"I know it's been a while," she said, and I almost laughed because a while is what you say when you haven't called someone in a month, not when you haven't spoken to them since you left a whole city and a whole life behind.

"It has," I said, keeping my voice flat, neutral, giving her nothing.

Her voice was the same. Soft but direct. Professional but with that little edge of familiarity that used to make me look up from my desk when she walked past. The kind of voice that used to say my name in a locked office in the basement of the old airline headquarters in Mount Prospect, the one nobody used anymore, the one I had the only key to because I headed the E-Verify project. The voice that used to whisper things I'm not going to repeat here because some things stay in the room they happened in.

"I need a favor," she said, and there it was. Of course she did. People don't call you after three years of silence because they miss you. They call because they need something.

"What kind of favor?"

"A driving job. Week-long gig. High-level clients in town for meetings between the Energy Corridor and Bush. They need someone professional. Someone discreet. Someone who knows Houston."

I didn't say anything for a second or two. Just let the silence sit there between us, heavy and awkward, the way silence sits when someone's asking you for something they know they don't have the right to ask for.

"You got my number after three years to book a ride?" I said jokingly.

"I got your number because I trust you," she said, and I heard the smile in her voice, that little lilt she used to use when she wanted something, the same tone she'd use when she'd text me at eleven forty-five in the morning with just a question mark and I'd know to meet her in fifteen minutes.

I didn't smile back. She couldn't see me, but I didn't smile.

"How many hours a day are they looking at?"

"Eighty-five an hour. Seventy plus hours guaranteed. Paid upfront. Cash if you want it, or I can wire it."

I did the math in my head. Seventy hours at $85 an hour was $5,950. That was real money, plus I'm sure they would have lunch and dinner, etc. This should be nice. The kind of money that makes you ignore who the call is coming from and rationalize past bad decisions and tell yourself it's just business.

"Who are the clients?"

"Energy sector. Executives from out of town. Meetings between corporate and regulatory offices. Nothing crazy. Just need a driver who knows Houston, knows how to navigate, and knows how to stay quiet."

"That's simple enough," I replied.

"I know," she said, and there was something in the way she said it that made my jaw tighten. "That's why I called you."

I should have said no. Should have told her I was booked. Should have hung up and blocked the number and gone back to scrolling my phone and waiting on my client who was now twenty minutes late and still texting apologies. But I didn't. Because part of me, some stupid, curious, reckless part, wanted to know why she really called. Wanted to know if it was really just about a driving job or if there was something else underneath it. Wanted to see if she still thought about that basement office the way I sometimes did when I couldn't sleep and my mind wandered back to Chicago and the version of me that used to sit on that desk twice a week while she locked the door.

"When?" I asked.

"Next week. Monday through Friday. I'll send details tonight. You in?"

I looked out the windshield at the Starbucks, at the people walking in and out with their drinks and their laptops and their problems that probably didn't include whether or not to take a job from someone who used to give you head in a locked room during lunch breaks while the rest of the office thought you were both out to lunch for a whole year.

"Yeah," I said. "I'm in."

"Thank you," she said, and then, quieter, almost like she didn't mean for me to hear it: "It's good to hear your voice."

I didn't say it back. Didn't say anything. But it was good to hear her voice too. I just hung up and sat there staring at my phone like it might explain what the hell I'd just agreed to.

My client finally showed up five minutes later, apologizing, out of breath, carrying three shopping bags and a coffee that was already half-empty. I smiled, said it was no problem, loaded her bags into the trunk, and drove her to the Galleria like nothing had happened. But the whole ride, I kept thinking about that voice. That call. That favor. And I kept telling myself it was just a job. Just money. Just five days of driving and then it'd be over and I'd never hear from her again.

I was wrong about that last part.

Monday evening I pulled up to a downtown high-rise off McKinney, one of those glass towers that reflects the sky so clean you can't tell where the building ends and the clouds begin. Valet out front, valets in matching vests, a place where parking costs more than some people's groceries for the week. I texted her to let her know I was outside, and a minute later three men stepped out through the revolving doors, looking like they owned not just the building but the block it sat on.

White men. Mid-forties to early fifties. Expensive suits that didn't wrinkle even in the Houston heat. Hair that looked like it had been styled twice that day. You know, super grip, extra mousse. Watches that caught the evening light and held it, flashing gold and silver like little signals of wealth. They moved with that kind of confidence you only get when you've never been told no, when every door you've ever walked toward has opened before you reached it, when the world has spent your whole life confirming that you matter more than other people.

One of them, tall, square jaw, graying temples, looked at me and nodded as he climbed into the backseat. Didn't say hello. Didn't introduce himself. Just nodded like I was supposed to know who he was.

"River Oaks," he said as he settled into the leather. "Steak dinner first. Then we'll see where the night takes us."

The other two laughed at that, one of them already scrolling his phone, the other cracking his knuckles and leaning back like he was settling in for a show.

I pulled out into traffic, smooth, no sudden moves, hands at ten and two like always. The city slid by in that golden-hour light, buildings glowing orange and pink, the kind of light that makes Houston look almost pretty if you squint and ignore the traffic and the heat and the fact that everything's trying to kill you.

They didn't acknowledge me after that. Just started talking like I wasn't there, like there was a soundproof partition between the front and back seats, even though there wasn't, like I was a piece of furniture that happened to move.

"Compliance is locked in," one of them said, the one in the middle, shorter than the others, with a voice that sounded like he smoked too much or yelled too much or both. "EPA's off our backs for another quarter at least."

"How'd you manage that?" the tall one asked, not looking up from his phone.

"Let's just say the right people got the right incentives," the short one said, and they all laughed, that kind of easy, careless laughter that comes when you think you're untouchable, when you think the rules don't apply to you because you've spent enough money to make sure they don't.

I kept my face neutral. Kept my eyes on the road. Kept my hands steady. But I was listening. I'm always listening. That's the job. That's what people forget. They think drivers are invisible. They think we don't matter. They don't know our pasts. They think we're too busy watching the road to pay attention to what's happening in the backseat.

They're wrong.

I pulled up to the restaurant, a steakhouse on West Gray, the kind of place where the menu doesn't have prices and the waiters call you sir even if you're twenty-two and wearing sneakers. I let them out, told them I'd be nearby, and parked half a block away where I could see the entrance.

They were inside for two hours. I know because I watched the clock the whole time, scrolling my phone, checking emails, wondering what they were talking about in there, wondering if Carla knew what kind of men she'd hired me to drive.

When they finally came out, they were louder. Looser. Ties undone, jackets slung over shoulders, laughing about something I couldn't hear. The tall one leaned into the window before getting in.

"You know any good spots?" he asked, and I knew what he meant. I knew exactly what he meant.

"Couple places," I said.

"Take us to the best one."

I drove them to a club in Midtown, one of those places with a private entrance around back, bottle service that costs more than rent, and women who will make a grown man cry to their momma and beg for forgiveness. I'd been there before, dropping off bachelor parties and corporate types and men who didn't want their wives to know where they were spending their Friday nights. I pulled up to the side door, the one without a line, the one with a bouncer who nodded at me like he recognized the truck, and let them out.

"You sure you don't want to come in?" one of them asked, grinning, half-drunk already. "We can get you in. On us."

"I'm good," I said. "I'll be out here."

They shrugged and walked inside, disappearing through the black door into the bass and the lights and whatever the hell they were about to spend the next three hours doing.

I parked across the street, engine off, windows cracked, and waited. That's most of the job, really. Waiting. People think driving is about driving, but it's not. It's about waiting. Waiting outside restaurants. Waiting outside clubs. Waiting outside hotels and offices and airports. Waiting while people live their lives and make their choices and do the things they don't want anyone to know about.

I scrolled my phone. Checked my messages. Watched the door.

Three hours later they came out, shirts untucked, ties gone completely now, eyes glassy and unfocused in that way that means they'd had too much of everything. One of them had lipstick on his collar, bright red, smudged. Another had a little white powder on the edge of his nostril that he didn't bother wiping off. They climbed in, still laughing, still talking, still acting like I wasn't there.

"Best night I've had in months," one of them said, slapping the seat.

"Wait till tomorrow," another one said. "We close the deal, and it's all downhill from there."

"Downhill?" the tall one said, leaning his head back against the leather. "More like offshore."

They all laughed at that, and I didn't know what it meant yet but

I filed it away in the back of my mind, the way I file away everything people say when they think I'm not listening.

I drove them back to their hotel, a Marriott downtown, sleek and expensive. They got out one by one, still laughing, still loud, and disappeared into the lobby. I sat there for a minute after they were gone, taking in the ride, staring at nothing. Then I put the truck in drive and went home.

Tuesday night was the same. Different restaurant, same energy. Same club, same chaos. Same conversations in the backseat, only this time they were less careful, more specific, more comfortable.

"Did you see the environmental impact report?" one of them asked.

"The one we submitted or the real one?" another said, and they all laughed.

"Doesn't matter," the tall one said. "They're not looking that close. They just want the signatures and the check."

"Especially the check," the short one added, and I watched them in the rearview, watched the way they smiled, the way they talked about regulations and reports and people's lives like it was all just a game, just numbers on a spreadsheet, just another deal to close.

I didn't say anything. Didn't react. I just drove. But I was starting to understand what kind of week this was going to be.

Wednesday night they were already drunk when I picked them up. One of them had a bottle of whiskey in some sort of silver canister, not a flask, but they were passing it around the backseat like high schoolers hiding from their parents.

"Where we going tonight, driver?" the tall one asked, and I told him wherever they wanted, and he liked that answer, told me I was smart, told me I knew how to play the game. Whatever the hell that meant, I thought.

They picked another club, fancier this time, more exclusive, the kind of place where you can't get in unless you know someone or you're rich enough that it doesn't matter if you know anyone. I dropped them off and parked just outside, and an hour later one of them came stumbling out to grab something from the car. He leaned against the window, phone in one hand, shirt half-open, smelling like Whiscolussy (whiskey, cologne, and pussy).

"You ever wonder what we do?" he asked, slurring just a little.

"Not my business," I said.

He grinned. "Smart man. That's the right answer."

He tapped the roof of the truck with his palm, making a dull thud that echoed in the quiet street.

"We're moving product," he said. "Waste, technically. Gotta put it somewhere, right? Can't just leave it sitting around waiting for the EPA to show up with clipboards and fines."

I didn't say anything. Just looked at him, waiting.

"EPA says we gotta process it a certain way," he continued, like he was explaining a simple concept to someone who didn't understand. "But processing costs money. Lots of money. So we streamline. Find cheaper options. Louisiana's got plenty of land nobody's using. Little bayou here, little plot there. Couple payments to the right people, and everybody's happy. Everybody wins."

"Streamline," I repeated, keeping my voice flat.

"Exactly," he said, pointing at me like I'd just answered a question correctly. "That's business, man. That's how you stay competitive. You cut costs where you can. You make the margins work."

He laughed, looked right at me, eyes glassy but focused enough to see me, to know I was there.

A few ticks later, the other men came out looking for the missing link. All three had quite the night, you could clearly tell.

"Where the fuck were you?" the tall one said in a stern voice, trying to get the truly wasted little one together.

"I was out there talking to the homey, my main man, my Ni-" He caught himself before he earned a broken jaw and a well whooped ass.

"I hope you haven't said anything you didn't have any business saying," the middle, kind of pudgy guy said gently.

"Who's gonna know, right?" he said. "The driver?"

The others cracked up at that, one of them slapping the seat, the other wiping tears from his eyes like it was the funniest thing he'd heard all week.

I didn't laugh. Didn't smile. Just sat there and drove, face neutral, eyes forward, like I hadn't heard a word.

When I arrived back to the hotel, the little one punched the roof, harder this time, and stumbled over a few words, laughing to himself, disappearing through the door like nothing had happened. The rest just got out and followed behind him, laughing, slumped and looking for the walls for support.

I sat there for a minute, alone in the truck, feeling the weight of what he'd just said settle into my chest. Then I started the engine, pulled off, and headed home for the night.

Thursday afternoon my phone rang while I was parked outside the men's business lunch. Carla's name lit up my screen. I stared at it for a second, debating whether to answer, then swiped to accept.

"How's it going?" she asked, and her voice sounded too casual, too light, like she was asking about the weather.

"Fine," I said.

"They treating you okay?"

"They're fine."

Pause. I could hear her breathing on the other end, could hear the slight hesitation before she spoke again.

"You hear anything... interesting?"

I stopped mid sip of my water. Looked at my phone like I could see her through it. "What kind of question is that?"

"Just asking," she said, but her voice had changed, gone from casual to careful, like she was testing me.

"Why?" I asked.

"No reason. Just making sure everything's smooth. Making sure they're not giving you any trouble."

"It's smooth," I said, and I could hear the edge in my own voice now, the suspicion creeping in.

"Good," she said. "That's good."

I hung up before she could say anything else. Sat there in my truck, staring at the phone in my hand, feeling that feeling that comes when you realize something's wrong but you can't quite name it yet. Some people call it their Spidey sense, some intuition. I call it WhoTheHellImAboutToFuckUp-ism.

She wasn't checking on me. She was checking on them. Making sure I was hearing what she wanted me to hear. Making sure I was close enough to whatever was happening that I'd be implicated if things went sideways.

I sat there for a long time, turning that thought over in my head, feeling the anger start to build somewhere deep, slow and steady like a fire catching.

Friday night, the last ride of the week, they were celebrating. The deal was closed, whatever that meant. Money was moving, they kept saying, like it was a living thing, like it had legs and a will of its own. Regulators were paid off. Everything was locked in. Everything was smooth.

Dinner that night was at a place I'd never heard of, some private dining room in a building that didn't have a sign, just a number on the door and a valet who looked at me like I didn't belong there. They were inside for four hours this time, and when they came out they were louder than they'd been all week, stumbling over each other, laughing so hard one of them couldn't catch his breath.

I drove them to the club one last time, waited while they disappeared inside, and picked them up at two in the morning when the place finally kicked them out. They could barely stand. One of them threw up in the bushes outside the entrance while the other two laughed and took pictures. I got them into the truck, one by one, making sure they didn't fall, making sure they didn't hurt themselves, because that's the job too, keeping people safe even when they don't deserve it.

I drove them back to the hotel, slow and steady, no sudden stops, no hard turns, just smooth and easy like I know to do. The tall one got out first, stumbling toward the lobby doors, mumbling something I couldn't understand. The other two followed, slapping each other on the back, laughing about something that probably wasn't funny.

I sat there a moment after they were gone, waiting to make sure they made it inside, waiting to make sure I didn't have to go chase anyone down.

That's when I noticed it.

A leather bag. On the floor of the backseat, half-hidden under the seat, like someone had kicked it there by accident. I looked toward the hotel lobby. They were gone. Already inside. Already on their way up to their rooms to pass out and forget this night ever happened.

I reached back and grabbed the bag.

It was heavy. Expensive leather, the kind that smells new even when it's not, the kind that costs more than most people make in a month. Monogrammed on the side in gold letters: SJH. Later, in the contracts, I saw the full name: Simon J. Hart.

I should have walked it inside. Should have handed it to the front desk, told them one of their guests left it in my car, and driven away clean.

But I didn't. Something told me not to. Something told me to look.

So I unzipped it.

And I looked.

Inside the bag was a laptop, sleek and black, the kind that costs three thousand dollars and comes with more security features than most people's houses. The screen was locked, password protected, a little white box glowing in the dark asking for credentials I didn't have. I did not touch the keyboard. Not one key.

Next to the laptop was a folder, thick, stuffed with papers, the edges bent like someone had been carrying it around for days, pulling things out and shoving them back in without caring how they looked.

I pulled the folder out and opened it.

Contracts. Printed emails. Spreadsheets with columns of numbers highlighted in yellow and pink, notes scribbled in the margins in handwriting I couldn't quite read. At the top of half the contracts, the same name kept showing up: Simon J. Hart.

The tall one. The one who never said hello.

I started flipping through, and the more I read, the tighter my chest got. Names. Dates. Locations. Offshore accounts in the Cayman Islands and the British Virgin Islands, accounts with numbers instead of names, accounts that didn't exist on any official record. Shell companies with addresses in Delaware and Nevada, companies that didn't make anything or sell anything, companies that existed just to move money from one place to another without anyone asking questions.

Payment schedules. Monthly deposits to officials in Louisiana, Texas, Mississippi. Names I recognized from the news, people who worked for the EPA, people who worked for state environmental agencies, people whose job it was to make sure companies like this one followed the rules.

And under all of that, buried near the bottom of the folder, two environmental impact reports.

Both with the same title, same date, same project name.

But the numbers were different.

One report, labeled "Submitted," showed contamination levels that were just barely within acceptable limits, numbers that would pass inspection, numbers that would get approved without anyone asking too many questions.

The other report, labeled "Internal Only," showed contamination levels fifty times higher. Levels that would shut the project down immediately. Levels that would trigger investigations and fines and lawsuits. Levels that would put people in prison if anyone ever saw them.

I sat there, staring at those two reports, feeling my heart pound in what seemed like my ears and feeling the weight of what I was holding settle into my hands like something alive.

Then I pulled out my phone and started taking pictures.

Every page. Every email. Every contract. Every highlighted number and every scribbled note. I didn't stop to think. Didn't stop to ask myself if this was the right move. I just shot. Click. Click. Click. The sound of the camera shutter filled the quiet truck and the low idle hum under the floorboards kept time.

When I finished with the folder, I reached back into the bag and pulled out the thumb drive. Small. Black. Unlabeled. I plugged it into my laptop, the one I keep in the front seat for navigation and paperwork and the occasional late-night Netflix binge when I'm waiting on a client who's taking too long.

The drive opened, and I saw folders. Dozens of them. More emails. More contracts. More spreadsheets. More evidence.

I didn't read through it all. Didn't have time. Just copied everything. Dragged the folders onto my desktop, watched the progress bar crawl across the screen, one percent, five percent, twenty percent, the laptop humming softly in the quiet.

It took four minutes. Four minutes that felt like an hour. Four minutes where I kept glancing at the hotel entrance, expecting one of them to come stumbling back out, expecting someone to knock on my window and ask what the hell I thought I was doing.

But no one came.

The transfer finished. I ejected the thumb drive, put it back in the bag, put the folder back, zipped everything up, and left the bag on the seat exactly where I'd found it.

Then I sat there, hands shaking, staring at my laptop screen, at the folders sitting there glowing in the dark, at the evidence I'd just taken from men who thought I was invisible.

I pulled out my phone and texted her.

"One of them left a bag. You want me to drop it at the desk?"

Three dots appeared immediately.

Then my phone rang.

"Where is it?" she said the second I answered. No hello. No pretense. Just panic, raw and unfiltered.

"In my car," I said.

"Did you look inside?"

I paused. Just long enough for her to understand.

"Did you fucking look inside?" she said again, louder now, voice cracking, and I could hear her moving, could hear a door close in the background like she'd gone somewhere private to have this conversation.

"Yeah," I said. "I looked."

Silence. Long and heavy. Then, quieter, almost a whisper: "What did you see?"

"Everything," I said.

More silence. I could hear her breathing, could hear the way it caught in her throat like she was trying not to cry or scream or both.

"Bring it to me," she said. "Now."

"It's two in the morning," I said.

"I don't care. Bring it to me. I'll text you an address. Just bring it."

"Why?" I asked. "What's in that bag that's got you this scared?"

"Just bring it," she said, and her voice broke completely now, all the control gone, all the professionalism stripped away, just fear underneath, raw and desperate.

"You set me up," I said.

The line went quiet. "What?"

"You called me for this job because you wanted me involved. You wanted me close to this. You wanted me to hear what they were saying, to see what they were doing, so that if shit went bad, you'd have someone to blame. Someone expendable. Someone who wouldn't fight back."

"That's not—"

"Don't lie to me," I said, and my voice was steady now, cold, the anger burning clean and focused. "You knew what kind of men these were. You knew what they were doing. And you called me because you thought I'd just drive. You thought I'd stay quiet. You thought I'd be the guy who was there when everything fell apart, the guy who could take the fall if they needed someone to pin it on."

Silence. Then: "I thought you'd just drive."

"And if things went bad, I'd be the one holding the bag. Literally."

She didn't deny it. Didn't argue. Just breathed into the phone, heavy and uneven.

"You set me up because I didn't want you," I said, and the words came out harder than I meant them to, sharper, cutting through whatever was left between us. "Three years ago. In that office. You wanted more. I didn't. And you never forgave me for that. So you called me down here, put me in a car with criminals, made sure I heard enough to be dangerous, and figured if everything went to hell, I'd be the one who went down for it. Not you. Not them. Me."

"Fuck you," she said, but her voice cracked on the second word, and I could tell she was crying now, could hear the tears she was trying to hold back.

"Yeah," I said. "Fuck me. But I'm keeping the bag."

"You can't,"

I hung up.

Sat there in the dark, phone in my hand, bag on the seat next to me, laptop glowing softly with folders full of evidence that could destroy lives, could end careers, could put people in prison for years.

I thought about calling her back. Thought about returning the bag and walking away clean, going back to my life, going back to driving people who didn't try to ruin me.

But then I thought about those men. Laughing in my backseat. Talking about dumping poison into land where people lived, where kids played, where families tried to build lives. Paying off regulators whose job it was to protect those people. Calling it streamlining. Calling it business. I thought about that motherfucker leaning against my window, grinning at me, asking who would know. The driver?

I thought about Carla, calling me after all these years, using my history, using the memory of what we did in that locked room to manipulate me into this.

And I made a decision.

I drove home, parked in my apartment lot, and carried my laptop inside. Sat at my dining table, the one that doubles as my office desk, and opened the folders I'd copied. Started reading through everything. Every email. Every contract. Every payment schedule. Every false report. I read until the sun came up. Read until my eyes burned. Read until I understood exactly what I was holding, exactly what these men had done, exactly how many laws they'd broken and how many people they'd hurt.

Then I opened a new email.

First recipient: FBI Environmental Crimes Unit, Houston field office. I'd looked up the address before I started, made sure it was real, made sure it would go to someone who could actually do something with it.

Subject line: Evidence of Illegal Waste Dumping and Regulatory Bribery.

I attached everything. Every file. Every folder. Every piece of evidence I'd copied. I sent from a clean account I set up that night. No signatures. No metadata that led back to me.

Then I wrote a note. Short. Direct. No emotion.

This is happening now. These are the people involved. These are the locations. These are the officials being paid off. Do your job.

I didn't sign it.

Then I opened a second email.

Recipient: an investigative journalist at the Houston Chronicle, someone who'd broken environmental stories before, someone I'd driven once who told me if I ever saw something worth sharing, I should call.

Subject line: Story You'll Want.

Same attachments. Same evidence. Different note this time.

These men are dumping toxic waste in Louisiana and paying off EPA officials to look the other way. This is real. This is happening now. This is your story.

Send.

Third email. EPA whistleblower hotline. Same files. Same evidence. Same message.

Send.

I closed my laptop. Sat there in the morning light, listening to the hum of the refrigerator, the distant sound of traffic outside, the quiet that comes after you've done something you can't take back.

Then I got dressed, got in my truck, and drove back to the hotel. Walked into the lobby like I owned the block, carrying the leather bag like it was mine, and set it on the front desk.

"One of your guests left this in my car last night," I told the clerk, a young guy with tired eyes and a name tag that said Marcus. "Which guest?"

"Tall guy. Gray hair. Expensive suit. Room's probably under the initials SJH."

"I'll make sure he gets it," Marcus said, taking the bag and setting it behind the desk.

"Appreciate it," I said.

Then I walked out, got back in my truck, and drove away.

Three weeks later I was sitting in my truck outside a Whole Foods, waiting on a client, scrolling through my phone, when I saw the headline.

Federal Investigation Launched into Energy Firm's Waste Disposal Practices.

I clicked the article. Read it twice. Names I recognized. Faces I'd driven. The tall one in handcuffs, walking into a federal building, head down, lawyers on either side. The short one refusing to comment, hand up to block the cameras.

And there, halfway down the article, buried in a paragraph about co-conspirators and ongoing investigations, her name, Carla. Indicted on charges of conspiracy, bribery, and falsifying federal documents.

I stared at her mugshot. Same face. Same eyes. But different now. Harder. Hollowed out. Like something inside her had broken and she was still trying to hold the pieces together.

I didn't feel vindicated. Didn't feel like I'd won anything. Didn't feel guilty either. Just felt done. Like a chapter had closed, and I didn't need to read it again.

I closed the article. Put my phone down. And went back to work.

Six months later, I was parked outside a coffee shop, waiting on a regular client who always tipped well and never asked too many questions, when my phone buzzed with an email.

From her.

Subject line: Why?

I stared at it for a second, thumb hovering over the delete button. Then I opened it.

Just one line inside.

"Why did you do it?"

I didn't respond. Just deleted it and went back to scrolling.

A week later, another email.

Subject: You ruined my life.

Deleted.

A month later, one more.

Subject: I hope you're happy.

I opened that one. Don't know why. Maybe just to see if there was anything left to say.

Inside, just one sentence.

"I gave you everything. And you destroyed me."

I read it twice. Then I hit reply. Typed one sentence back.

"You gave me fifteen minutes a day in a basement and a setup that could've destroyed me. I gave you a choice. You made yours. I made mine."

Send.

She never wrote back after that. I never expected her to.

A year later I was driving someone else, some corporate type heading to the airport, talking on the phone about quarterly earnings and market projections, when I passed the high-rise where I'd picked up those men that first night. The building looked the same. Glass reflecting the sky. Valets in their vests. People walking in and out like nothing had ever happened there.

I didn't slow down. Didn't stop. Just drove past and kept going.

But I thought about that week. About the men who thought I didn't matter. About the woman who thought I'd protect her because we had history. About the choice I made to stop being silent when silence would've been easier.

And I didn't regret it. Not the sending or the evidence. Not the phone call or the emails or the way it all played out.

Because some people mistake silence for weakness. Some people think quiet means complicit. Some people think that because you don't talk, you don't think.

They're wrong.

I'm the Silent Driver. I see everything. I hear everything. I remember everything.

But silence isn't loyalty. It's not protection. It's strategy. And when the strategy changes, so do I.

I kept driving. Kept picking up strangers. Kept listening to their stories. Kept staying quiet when they needed me to.

But I also kept those files on my laptop, backed up, encrypted, just in case. Because you never know when someone's going to try to use you again. You never know when silence stops being a choice and starts being a trap.

And I learned something that week that I'll never forget.

The people who think you're invisible are the ones who should be watching you the closest.

Because the quiet ones, we're the ones who see everything. We're the ones who know where the bodies are buried. We're the ones who decide when to speak.

And when we do, we don't whisper.

People think guilt screams. It doesn't. It hums, low and steady, somewhere between the tires and the truth. But this time I didn't hear it. Not for her. Not for them. Not for any of it.

Because I didn't stay silent to protect anyone. I stayed silent long enough to act. And when I acted, I didn't do it halfway.

Some people hire you to drive them somewhere. Some people hire you to be their alibi. Some people hire you thinking you'll stay quiet because of what happened between you in a room that doesn't exist anymore.

They're wrong.

Silence isn't forever. And when it breaks, it breaks loud.

After that week, I saw different clients, same routine. I'd pick people up, take them where they needed to go, and listen to whatever they said in the backseat. Most of the time their secrets were small, complaints about their boss, arguments with their spouse, things they wouldn't say out loud anywhere else. I kept those secrets because there was no reason not to.

But I was different after that. More careful. I started checking bags before I returned them. Kept my phone charged, my laptop backed up. I stopped taking jobs from people I used to know, stopped trusting voices that sounded too familiar, especially when they called after years of silence asking for something simple.

Because nothing's ever simple.

I thought about her sometimes. Late at night when the roads were empty and my mind had nowhere else to go. I wondered if she blamed me for everything, or if she'd figured out by now that I was just the last piece in something she'd set in motion herself.

I wondered if she ever thought about that basement office. The locked door. The way she'd look at me afterward like she wanted to say something but never did.

I didn't do it because I hated her. I did it because she tried to use me. Because she thought fifteen minutes of attention years ago bought my silence forever.

She was wrong.

A few months later, I got a text from a number I didn't recognize. Just five words: You were always too smart.

I stared at it for a while, trying to figure out if it was her, if it was a compliment or a threat. Then I deleted it and moved on.

Because staying quiet doesn't keep you safe. It just keeps you invisible. And invisible men don't get to choose what happens to them.

I drove past the old Airline building about a year after everything went down. I was in Chicago for a family thing and found myself near Mount Prospect, near the headquarters that used to be my whole world.

The building looked smaller than I remembered. Older. Like it had aged the same way I had.

I didn't stop. Just drove past slow, looking at the windows, wondering if she ever thought about that place the way I sometimes did.

Probably not. She'd probably rewritten the story by now, convinced herself I was the villain and she was the victim.

People do that. Rewrite their own history until they can live with it.

I do it too. The difference is I know I'm doing it.

The story I tell myself, the one where I stopped the bad guys and did the right thing, isn't the whole truth. The truth is simpler. I didn't do it to save her, and I didn't do it out of anger. I did it because once I saw what was in that folder, I couldn't unsee it. Because people were going to get hurt, and silence would've made me part of it. Some things you don't walk away from. Not if you want to recognize yourself the next morning.

That night with the murderer in Montrose, when I stayed quiet because speaking up would've destroyed me, I made the only choice I could. My silence was survival.

But this time was different. This time I had the evidence. I had proof. I had the power to make people listen without putting myself in danger.

This time my silence wasn't survival. It was strategy.

I stayed quiet long enough to gather what I needed. Long enough to understand what I was looking at. And when I spoke, I did it with their words, their evidence, their files, the ones they left behind because they thought I was too insignificant to matter.

That's the difference between being silenced and being silent. Being silenced means someone took your voice. Being silent means you're choosing when to use it.

People asked me sometimes if I ever thought about getting out. Going back to corporate, using my degree, finding something that didn't involve traffic and strangers.

The answer was always no.

Not because I loved driving. But because behind this wheel, I got to see people for who they really were. I got to hear the truth underneath the lies. And I got to make the choice that mattered, silence or voice, complicity or action.

In an office somewhere, I'm just another employee. Another name on a list.

But in this truck, I'm the one with the power. I'm the one who decides what happens next.

So I kept driving. Kept listening. Kept choosing when to stay quiet and when to speak up. When to keep a secret and when to break it.

And every time I made that choice, I thought about that week. About those men and that woman and that bag full of evidence. About the moment I decided to stop being invisible.

I don't regret it. Not for a second.

Because some people think silence is weakness. They think quiet means harmless. They think that because you don't talk, you don't matter.

They're wrong.

And when they figure that out, when the handcuffs click and the headlines break and they're sitting somewhere wondering who talked, they'll never know it was me.

The driver. The guy they ignored. It's not that you never speak. It's that when you do, nobody sees it coming.

SIXTEEN
THE CHARTER

I pulled up to the JW Marriott downtown a little before noon, It was a cool and wet Saturday afternoon after a torrential downpour of rain. A rain that came out of nowhere. Now there is just an orange haze of sorts over the city. The damn weatherman said that it was going to be clear skies and no rain. I still don't understand why those dudes get paid.

I eased the bus to the curb, checked my mirrors, and let the engine idle while I grabbed my phone to create my sign. It read The Legacy Group22 in clean black letters across a white background. I don't usually need to make signs since I know most of my clients, but when I do, I am grateful for the BIG app. I don't usually drive buses either. But when the booking came through online - thirty-passenger charter, deposit paid in full, the name Legacy staring at me next to the number twenty-two; I couldn't hand it off. You know me and numbers. Proverbs 13:22 been my north star for years. I took it as a sign and told Mike I'd handle it myself.

Mike's owns his own limo service and he just got a small charter bus. The bus was bigger than anything I'd driven. Still smelled new, leather seats tight, faint echo when you talked. He'd told me no driver was free that day, but I could take it if I wanted. Thinking of the liability I was hesitant, but something in me said this one mattered. So I wiped down everything, checked the gas, and prepped the cabin with my Legacy details, custom water bottles, napkins, etc.

When I stepped outside with the sign in hand, I straightened my shirt, leaned against the bus door, and waited. People passed with their rolling bags and conference lanyards, like little school kids with their names posted around their necks. I looked down at the sign again and whispered to myself, "Legacy Group22."

Then I saw a familiar face coming out of the front door.

"Mr. David's son?" I said before I could stop myself.

He looked up, smiled like he'd been expecting me. "Hey, what's up, Mr. Otis son? I'm the guest speaker at the conference you're taking us to."

"The conference?"

"Yeah. Legacy Group event. Your dad here too."

My mouth went dry. "My Dad?"

He nodded toward the doors, and before I could ask another question, I saw him, My dad himself, dressed I his clean business suit, dark shades and a book in his hand. He shook my hand and said his hello's. Then said man you got me out here networking and started to laugh. We all laughed as he got on the bus. Behind him came Mrs. Pinkerman, came out with a pants suit sharp as razers. She looked at me, slowly tilted her head down and whispered, I'm sorry if I caused a stain.

So you know I'm thinking what the fuck is going on here. Then Mr. Kraken shuffled out, frail but steady, like he'd been waiting on this ride for longer than any of us. "You can't get rid of me that easy" he stated as I assisted him on the bus. He was frail, but he looked surprisingly good.

Next was the man I never wanted to see again, that motherfucker who I know killed his wife and used me as an alibi. The Murderer. He wore a dark suit this time, clean-cut, no blood on his hands, eyes down like he was sorry. I should pat this motherfucker down, ain't no telling what his ass is hiding.

Ok, this has to be some sick ass joke. Is this like a this is your life moment like they use to do back in the day? Or some kind of Punk'd bullshit because this is starting to freak me out. Am I fucking dead? What's really going on?

Behind him was Lang Jang, still talking on two phones at once, screaming I'm sick of you cock suckers. What? I though? He has lost his mind or did I?

Then, Michelle, Michelle? But I thought... looking better than the last time I saw her. You tried to kill me? Really? I can't believe you would pull that bullshit.

Finally, a pleasant face, the Hogans, oh we are so glad you are doing well. You look so handsome Mrs. Hogan said.

Then my coworker from the airline, the silent passenger, the woman in the red dress, Marcus, Mr. Richardson, the lawyers, they came one after another, each greeting me like old friends boarding for a trip we'd planned years ago.

As I got on the bus, I heard a bang at the front of the JW doors. Big Sip, came running into the sliding door yelling, You motherfuckers better not leave me. My fat ass needs a ride and I'm tired.

This has got to be the strangest trip of my life. I can't explain it.

After Big Sip climbs his ass on the bus, I close the door. And get ready to pull off.

Mr. David's son, says No, we have a few more. Now I turn around to him and look him in the eyes and say, if my mother come out that fucking door, I'm kicking your ass, I promise you.

Confused, he said I don't know your mother. Didn't you say that she passed away years ago. I could have sworn I sent you flowers. Yes, you did I'm sorry Mr. David's son. I guess I just have a lot on my mind. But I didn't, I just didn't understand what was happening.

We have musical guests preforming at the venue today... Oh here they come now.

First came Sudnalro Soul, this motherfucker wasn't even walking it was like he was gliding to the bus, like he was in an old school Spike Lee Joint gliding across the screen. How did this know it was going to be a chilly day, his ass had on a velvet suit sat in the back corner, head tilted, humming some slow jam that didn't exist yet.

Deacon came leaned against the bus near the middle row, hat tipped low, the gold cross at his neck catching the light. Dressed in his Country boots, finishing up his drink. Then said, I'm waiting on the boss man.

Solin.Star moved with energy, graceful and had a glow to her. She left a trail of glitter behind her. She sat on the bus eyes closed, earphones glowing faintly pink, like she was listening to the sound of her own thoughts.

Mind of Malachi was a group of singers, not a choir but a collective. They all moved like a movement, collectively and with purpose. Each one had a notebook open, pen scratching fast, lips moving without sound.

The Sutradhar was mystical. Walking with some sort of wrap on and sandals, he sat quietly near the front, he was weaving together what looked like a scroll of some sort. He had a commanding presence and never said a word.

The Kid, a small dude that didn't say anything but kept fucking smiling at me. I know he had to be hot wearing that damn costume. He sat in the front row, legs swinging, with a glowing heart effect glowing through his orange sweater.

And the last dude wasn't wearing a lanyard; he looked familiar but I couldn't place him. He had an aura about himself. Tall, bald, and had a beard, wearing a tailored black suit and shoes that shined and looked like glass. He got on and said we can go now. Not like ok we are all here but like he was giving a command. And for some reason, I listened.

The air changed, it wasn't cold or warm, just heavy. The kind of heavy that makes you wonder if the world's holding its breath. I closed the door, checked the mirrors again, and said, LEGACY, L.E.T.S. Roll.

They all said in unison, You're in Control.

I put the bus in gear and eased onto Main Street. Downtown slid by in slow motion. Buildings looked taller, shadows longer. I glanced at the rearview mirror and caught glimpses of everyone, their reflections didn't always match their bodies. The murderer's reflection looked like a boy in church clothes. Mrs. Pinkerman's reflection was a young woman in a sundress. Michelle's was laughing, head thrown back, like death never touched her.

The further we drove, the quieter it got. City noise faded until all I could hear was the low hum of the engine and the faint rhythm of Sudnalro's humming.

Then the orange haze or fog entered the bus.

At the first red light, I looked down and saw the gas gauge needle twitch, like the bus was alive. The GPS blinked "Route recalculating," even though I hadn't entered a destination. I tapped it, but it stayed blank except for one word: Legacy.

I laughed under my breath. "Alright then."

We rolled on.

The streets started to change. Skyscrapers melted into trees, sidewalks turned to dirt, and I swear the air itself started to shimmer like heat waves on asphalt. I checked the mirror again. Every face stared straight ahead, calm, waiting.

I wanted to ask questions, but something told me to just drive. I couldn't speak, it was like I was being gagged

When I glanced in the side mirror again, the skyline was gone completely. Behind us was open sky and nothing else. No road, no buildings, no sound. Just the hum of the tires on something that looked like pavement but didn't feel real.

Then voices started blending. Not loud, not chaotic just low murmurs weaving together like background music.

Mrs. Pinkerman was moaning again. Mr. Kraken was shitting an on himself or it smelled like it. The lawyers argued softly over nothing. Michelle was laughing with the silent passenger, I thought that bastard didn't speak. The murderer was whispering apologies to no one.

And over all of it, the musicians began speaking like narrators layered over each other.

Sudnalro said, "Love don't leave, it changes form."

Deacon said, "She's too beautiful to burn."

Solin whispered, "Everything is frequency."

Malachi murmured scripture without words.

The Sutradhar recorded in silence.

The kid giggled softly and the whole bus flickered, light pulsing with the sound.

Where is that other motherfucker? Where did he go?

I gripped the wheel tighter. "Y'all feel that?"

No one answered.

The hum grew louder. Lights from the dashboard began to pulse with the same rhythm as The kid's glow. The speedometer needle floated past numbers that didn't make sense.

I blinked. For a split second, I wasn't behind the wheel, I was sitting in the back, watching myself drive. Or maybe I was in every seat at once. The murderer's voice came through like an echo. "You always was the driver, weren't you?"

I tried to speak but the words came out doubled, layered with someone else's voice.

I looked down at my hands on the wheel. They weren't the same. One looked older, one younger, one darker, one lighter. Every version of me flickered through like bad reception.

"Where the fuck are we going?" I gasped

Sudnalro smiled in the mirror. "Home."

Deacon said, "Wherever that is."

The bus shook once, like turbulence, then steadied. The outside world looked like watercolor now, shapes bleeding into light. The passengers didn't seem bothered. They were fading at the edges but still talking, still smiling.

Mrs. Pinkerman reached across the aisle and held the murderer's hand. Lang Jang hung up both his phones and started screaming Lang Jang scared than a motherfucker, I think Lang Jang about to shit himself too. Mr. Kraken closed his eyes and whispered, "About time."

Big Sip yelled "Oh, you shitting me? Y'all better let me off this motherfucker! I can't believe you got me up in this bullshit."

The road ahead turned gold.

I wanted to slow down but the pedal moved on its own. The speedometer blinked zero even as we moved faster. I felt weightless, like gravity had forgotten me.

The bus wasn't metal anymore. It was light, threads of it wrapping around every passenger like they were woven together. Faces blurred, shapes merged, colors dissolved.

I blinked again and saw every story I'd ever told, every ride, every lie, every truth, playing across the windshield like a movie.

The murderer holding his child.

Mrs. Pinkerman dancing naked in her kitchen.

Deacon laying under an oak tree.

Sudnalro singing on a rooftop.

Solin painting light with her hands.

Malachi writing a verse that glowed on the page.

The kid's little heart shining brighter than the sun.

Where is that fucking dude.... I know ya'll seen him. What the fuck did he do?

Each image flashed, bright then gone.

I opened my mouth to say something but the sound that came out wasn't mine. It was all of theirs, every passenger, every voice I'd ever borrowed, speaking through me in one tone that sounded like wind and thunder mixed.

And then, BAM

I don't know what, and I won't pretend I do.

But when I opened my eyes, the bus wasn't there. Neither were they.

I was sitting on my couch, remote in hand, TV flickering. My heart was racing like I'd just driven through a storm.

On the screen, a voice said, "Some stories you believe. Some you don't. And some... believe you."

I looked at the corner of the screen; Ripley's Believe It or Not. Or maybe The Twilight Zone. The colors kept changing like the signal couldn't decide. I looked down and saw empty bags of Flamin' Hots.

Those damn Flamin' Hots. I don't know why I keep eating that shit.

I leaned back, trying to remember if I'd fallen asleep. My phone buzzed on the coffee table.

I reached to grab it and felt something heavy around my neck.

I looked down.

A lanyard.

Black cord. Plastic badge holder. And inside, a card that said: **The Legacy Group, Orlandus Shorter.**

What the fuck?

I pulled it off, turned it over in my hands. I wasn't wearing this when I sat down.

Was I?

My phone buzzed again.

I looked at the screen.

A new booking request.

Name: **The Legacy Group22**.

Deposit: Paid in full.

I stared at the lanyard in my hand. Then at the screen. Then back at the lanyard.

Then I laughed.

Aww HELL NAW

Ain't NO FUCKING WAY!

ACKNOWLEDGMENTS

My deepest thanks to everyone who trusted me with their stories, and to everyone who stood beside me while I found my voice.

To my brother, **DeHaven** — without you, these stories would've been totally made up. You helped turn the vision into reality, and I am forever grateful.

To **Nikki White-Shepard** (RIP) — thank you for encouraging me to use my words. You saw something in me that many did not, and I appreciate you for being the woman you were. I am forever honored to have been able to call you, my friend. "Hallmark" is on it.

To **every passenger** of Legacy Executive Transportation Services, LLC — each of you made this happen. A piece of each of you stuck with me. It was an honor to be of service to every one of you. Thank you for being part of the Legacy ETS family and for trusting me to be a carrier of your secrets.

Special thank you to **Michael Shorter** — your support in every path I've taken is immeasurable. Thank you for always showing up.

To my **Pastor, Keion Henderson** — thank you for your teachings. Although I never told you how much you helped change my life personally, I hope this shines as bright as the ideas and insight you've given me over the years.

And finally, to **every hater, naysayer, and nonbeliever** — I appreciate your methods. You proved to be fuel to keep the fire within burning. Don't worry… I'll have more shit for you to talk about. Count on it. That's a promise.

ABOUT THE AUTHOR

Orlandus Shorter was born in Jackson, Mississippi, and raised on Chicago's West Side. He started writing young: songs, poems, and journal entries. But somewhere along the road, life got louder than his words. Family, responsibilities, and survival took the front seat, and writing quietly rode in the back. Years later, while working as a limousine driver, he began to notice the stories happening around him. The laughter, secrets, heartbreak, and silence of the people he drove night after night reminded him of what he'd lost. Slowly, urgently, he started writing again. When the world shut down, Orlandus shifted gears by earning his CDL and taking to the open highway as a truck driver. Long nights on the interstate gave him the space to think, pray, and put his truth back into words. What began as a reflection became The Silent Driver, a blend of stories inspired by the people he'd carried.

He continues to create from Houston, Texas, still writing between miles, still building, and still chasing vision one story at a time.

Learn more at www.orlandusshorter.com or follow \@Orlandus.Shorter

If this story moved you, I'd love to hear from you.

Leave a review online or share a note about which chapter

stayed with you the most. Your voice helps stories like these
find new passengers.

ALSO BY ORLANDUS SHORTER

The Silent Driver Soundtrack

Available now on all streaming platforms

Stream the soundtrack on Apple Music, Spotify, Amazon Music,

YouTube Music or visit

www.orlandusshorter.com

R&B artist Sudnalro Soul creates music that feels intimate, emotional, and deeply human. His sound blends slow-burn soul, grown R&B, and heartfelt storytelling that lives in the tension between desire and vulnerability. Sudnalro leans into raw feeling, honest reflection, and the kind of love songs that hit harder the more you've lived. Every track is crafted with attention, every lyric carries weight, and the music reflects a man who understands passion, loss, romance, and redemption.

@SudnalroSoul

Country-Soul Blues artist DEACON carries the grit of Port Gibson, Mississippi, the warmth of Southern gospel, and the storytelling power of a man who's lived every mile he sings. His music is rooted, grown, and honest — shaped by faith, struggle, and the kind of life experience you can't fake. Deacon is building moments that feel real. Every song stands on its own, every line comes from somewhere true, and the music speaks exactly the way he intends it to.

@officialdeaconmusic

Glowkka™ is a gentle, glowing quokka from a hidden valley in the Outback — a magical companion created to bring comfort, courage, and kindness to children and families. With his burnt-orange sweater and shining heart, Glowkka communicates through expression, movement, and the warmth he carries. His world is built on wonder, healing, and emotional safety. Through stories, songs, affirmations, and adventures with his light-themed friends, Glowkka helps children navigate feelings, face challenges, and remember that they are never alone. Every Glowkka project is created with softness, heart, and imagination.

@Glowkka

Mind of Malachi

Mind of Malachi is a contemplative voice rooted in faith, scripture, and the real walk with God. The work blends prayer, poetry, and raw honesty — speaking directly to those living between promise and fulfillment, joy and struggle, faith and doubt. Malachi doesn't offer clichés or easy answers. Every song, reflection, and devotional is shaped by lived experience, spiritual weight, and a desire to help people see God clearly in the middle of real life. The message is the mission, and the mission is to reach the ones who feel overlooked in the journey

@TheMindofMalachi

Solin.Star blends cosmic ambiance, alt-R&B textures, and hypnotic melodic storytelling. Her sound is ethereal but grounded, shining with shimmering synths, deep emotion, and the pull of a woman who feels everything and says only what matters. Solin.Star builds worlds instead of songs — galaxies of desire, introspection, vulnerability, and freedom. She is the quiet storm and the bright pulse at the same time. Her music reaches places beyond genre, guided by intuition, atmosphere, and emotional truth.

@Solin.Star

Orlandus Shorter

THE SUTRADHAR

Orlandus Shorter is a storyteller, creator, and builder of worlds. From music to books to cinematic concepts, his work centers on legacy, purpose, and the quiet truths that shape a man. He's been a graphic designer, truck driver, limousine driver, and Human Resources professional—roles that taught him to observe, listen, and create with intention.
As the founder of The Legacy Group, Orlandus moves with clarity and discipline. Whether composing instrumentals, writing stories, crafting songs, or developing new ideas, his mission is singular: to leave something meaningful behind. He creates for generations he may never meet.

@Orlandus.Shorter

If this story moved you, I'd love to hear from you. Leave a review online or share a note about which chapter stayed with you the most. Your voice helps stories like these find new passengers.

Thank you for riding with me.

9 781970 955002